Mitchell approached on soundless stockinged feet.

The two men swung round in remarkably swift unison, hands reaching for their guns. It was too late. The deep-bluish sheen of Mitchell's silencer-equipped .38 was very visible.

"Clasp your hands behind your necks, turn round and start walking," said Mitchell.

They walked until they could walk no more, for the good reason that they had reached the end of the platform.

"You're the two who gunned down Melinda and Mr. Roomer?"

There was no reply. Mitchell squeezed the trigger twice and was walking away before the dead men had hit the waters of the Gulf. He had taken only four steps when a flashlight beam struck him in the face. He couldn't see the man——or the gun behind the flashlight.

"Now it's my turn," said a voice.

Fawcett Books
by Alistair MacLean:

H.M.S. ULYSSES

THE GUNS OF NAVARONE

SOUTH BY JAVA HEAD

THE SECRET WAYS

NIGHT WITHOUT END

FEAR IS THE KEY

THE BLACK SHRIKE

THE GOLDEN RENDEZVOUS

THE SATAN BUG

ICE STATION ZEBRA

WHEN EIGHT BELLS TOLL

WHERE EAGLES DARE

FORCE 10 FROM NAVARONE

PUPPET ON A CHAIN

CARAVAN TO VACCARES

BEAR ISLAND

THE WAY TO DUSTY DEATH

BREAKHEART PASS

CIRCUS

THE GOLDEN GATE

SEAWITCH

SEAWITCH

Alistair MacLean

FAWCETT CREST • NEW YORK

SEAWITCH

THIS BOOK CONTAINS THE COMPLETE TEXT
OF THE ORIGINAL HARDCOVER EDITION

Published by Fawcett Crest Books, a unit of CBS Publications,
the Consumer Publishing division of CBS Inc.,
by arrangement with Doubleday and Company, Inc.

ISBN: 0-449-23597-1

Alternate Selection of the Literary Guild, August 1977

Printed in the United States of America

10 9 8 7 6 5 4 3 2 1

SEAWITCH

Prologue

NORMALLY there are only two types of marine machines concerned with the discovery and recovery of oil from under the ocean floor. The first, mainly engaged in the discovery of oil, is a self-propelled vessel, sometimes of very considerable size. Apart from its towering drilling derrick, it is indistinguishable from any oceangoing cargo vessel; its purpose is to drill boreholes in areas where seismological and geological studies suggest oil may exist. The technical operation of this activity is highly complex, yet these vessels have achieved a remarkable level of success. However, they suffer from two major drawbacks. Although they are equipped with the most advanced and sophisticated navigational equipment, including bowthrust propellers, for them to maintain position in running seas, strong tides and winds when boring can be extremely difficult, and in really heavy weather operations have to be suspended.

For the actual drilling of oil and its recovery—principally its recovery—the so-called "jack-up system" is in almost universal use. This system has to be towed into position, and consists basically of a platform which carries the drilling rig, cranes, helipads and all essential services, including living accommodations, and is attached to the seabed by firmly anchored legs. In normal conditions it is extremely effective, but like the discovery ships it has drawbacks. It is not mobile. It has to suspend operations in even moderately heavy weather. And it can be used only in comparatively shallow water: the deepest is in the North Sea, where most of those rigs are to be found. This North Sea rig stands in about 450 feet of water, and the cost of increasing the length of those legs would be so prohibitive as to make oil recovery quite uneconomical, even though Americans have plans to construct a rig with 800-foot legs off the California Coast. There is also the unknown safety factor. Two such rigs have already been lost in the North Sea. The cause of those disasters has not been clearly evaluated, although it is suspected, obviously not without basis, that there may have been design, structural or metallic faults in one or more of the legs.

And then there is the third type of oil rig—the TLP—technically, the tension leg drilling/production platform. At the time of this story there was only one of its type in the world. The platform, the working area, was about the size of a football field—if, that is, one can imagine a triangular football field, for the platform was, in fact, an equilateral triangle. The deck was not made of steel but of a uniquely designed ferro-concrete, specially developed by a Dutch ship-building company. The supports for this massive platform had been designed and built in England and consisted of three enormous steel legs, each at one corner of the structure, the three being joined together by a variety of horizontal and diagonal hollow cylinders, the total combination offering such tremendous buoyancy that the working platform they supported was out of reach of even the highest waves.

From each of the bases of the three legs, three massive steel cables extended to the base of the ocean floor, where each triple set was attached to large sea-floor anchors. Powerful motors could raise or lower these cables, so that the anchors could be lowered to a depth two or three times that of most modern fixed oil derricks, which meant that this rig could operate at depths far out on the continental shelf.

The TLP had other very considerable advantages.

Its great buoyancy put the anchor cables under constant tension, and this tension practically eliminated the heaving, pitching and rolling of the platform. Thus the rig could continue operating in very severe storms, storms that would automatically stop production on any other type of derrick.

It was also virtually immune to the effects of an undersea earthquake.

It was also mobile. It had only to up anchors and move to potentially more productive areas.

And compared to standard oil rigs, its cost of establishing position in any given spot was so negligible as to be worth no more than a passing mention.

The name of the TLP was *Seawitch*.

Chapter 1

*I*N certain places and among certain people, the *Seawitch* was a very bad name indeed. But, overwhelmingly, their venom was reserved for a certain Lord Worth, a multi—some said bulti—millionaire, chairman and sole owner of North Hudson Oil Company and, incidentally, owner of the *Seawitch*. When his name was mentioned by any of the ten men present at that shoreside house on Lake Tahoe, it was in tones of less than hushed reverence.

Their meeting was announced in neither the national nor local press. This was due to two factors. The delegates arrived and departed either singly or in couples, and among the heterogeneous summer population of Lake Tahoe such comings and goings went unremarked or were ignored. More importantly, the delegates to the meeting were understandably reluctant that their assembly become common knowledge. The day was Friday the thirteenth, a date that boded no good for someone.

There were nine delegates present, plus their host. Four of them mattered, but only two seriously—Corral, who represented the oil and mineral leases in the Florida area, and Benson, who represented the rigs off Southern California. Of the other six, only two mattered. One was Patinos of Venezuela; the other, known as Borosoff, of Russia, whose interest in American oil supplies could only be regarded as minimal. It was widely assumed among the others that his only interest in attending the meeting was to stir up as much trouble as possible, an assumption that was probably correct.

All ten were, in various degrees, suppliers of oil to the United States and had one common interest: to see that the price of those supplies did not drop. The last thing they all wanted to see was an oil-value depreciation.

Benson, whose holiday home this was and who was nominally hosting the meeting, opened the discussion.

"Gentlemen, does anyone have any objections if I bring a third party—that is, a man who represents neither ourselves nor Lord Worth—into this meeting?"

Practically everyone had, and there were some moments of bedlamic confusion: they had not only objections but very strong ones at that.

Borosoff, the Russian, said: "No. It is too dangerous." He glanced around the group with calculated suspiciousness. "There are already too many of us privy to these discussions."

Benson, who had not become head of one of Europe's biggest oil companies, a British-based one, just because someone had handed him the job as a birthday present, could be disconcertingly blunt.

"You, Borosoff, are the one with the slenderest claims to be present at this meeting. You might well bear that in mind. Name your suspect." Borosoff remained silent. "Remember, gentle-men, the objective of this meeting—to maintain, at least, the present oil-price levels. The OPEC is now actively considering hiking the oil prices. That doesn't hurt us much here in the U.S.— we'll just hike our own prices and pass them on to the public."

Patinos said: "You're every bit as unscrupulous and ruthless as you claim us to be."

"Realism is not the same as ruthlessness. Nobody's going to hike anything while North Hudson is around. They are already undercutting us, the majors. A slight pinch, but we feel it. If we raise our prices more and his remain steady, the slight pinch is going to increase. And if he gets some more TLPs into operation, then the pinch will begin to hurt. It will also hurt the OPEC, for the demand for your products will undoubtedly fall off.

"We all subscribe to the gentlemen's agreement among major oil companies that they will not prospect for oil in international waters—that is to say, outside their own legally and internationally recognized territorial limits. Without observance of this agreement, the possibilities of legal, diplomatic, political and international strife, ranging from scenes of political violence to outright armed confrontation, are only too real. Let us suppose that Nation A—as some countries have already done—claims all rights for all waters a hundred miles offshore from its coasts. Let us further suppose that Nation B comes along and starts drilling thirty miles outside those limits. Then let us suppose that Nation A makes a unilateral decision to extend its offshore limits to a hundred and fifty miles—and don't forget that Peru has claimed two hundred miles as its limits: the subsequent possibilities are too awesome to contemplate.

"Alas, not all are gentlemen. The chairman of the North Hudson Oil Company, Lord Worth, and his entire pestiferous board of directors would have been the first to vehemently deny any suggestion that they were gentlemen, a fact held in almost universal acceptance by their competitors in oil. They would also have denied equally vehemently that they were criminals, a fact that may or may not have been true, but it most certainly is not true now.

"He has, in short, committed two of what should be indictable offenses. 'Should,' I say. The first is unprovable; the second, although an offense in moral terms, is not, as yet, strictly illegal.

"The facts of the first—and what I consider much the minor offense—concerns the building of Lord Worth's TLP in Houston. It is no secret in the industry that the plans were stolen—those for the platform from the Mobil Oil Company, those for the legs and anchoring systems from the Chevron Oilfield Research Company. But, as I say, unprovable. It is commonplace for new inventions and developments to occur at two or more places simultaneously, and he can always claim that his design team, working in secret, beat the others to the punch."

Benson was perfectly correct. In the design of the *Seawitch* Lord Worth had adopted shortcuts which the narrow-minded could have regarded as unscrupulous, if not illegal. Like all oil companies, North Hudson had its own design team. They were all cronies of Lord Worth, employed solely for tax-deduction purposes; their combined talents would have been incapable of designing a rowboat.

This did not worry Lord Worth. He had no need for a design team. He was a vastly wealthy man, had powerful friends—none of them, needless to say, among the oil companies—and was a master of industrial espionage. With these resources at his disposal, he found little trouble in obtaining those two secret advance plans, which he passed on to a firm of highly competent marine designers, whose exorbitant fees were matched only by their extreme discretion. The designers found little difficulty in marrying the two sets of plans, adding just sufficient modifications and improvements to discourage those with a penchant for patent-rights litigation.

Benson went on: "But what really worries me, and what should worry all you gentlemen here, is Lord Worth's violation of the tacit agreement never to indulge in drilling in international waters." He paused, deliberately for effect, and looked slowly at each of the other nine in turn. "I say in all seriousness, gentlemen, that Lord Worth's foolhardiness and greed may well prove to be the spark that triggers a third world war. Apart from protecting our own interests, I maintain that for the good of mankind—and I speak from no motive of spurious self-justification—if the governments of the world do not intervene, then it is imperative that we should. As the governments show no sign of intervention, then I suggest that the burden lies upon us. This madman must be stopped. I think you gentlemen would agree that only we realize the full implications of all of this and that only we have the technical expertise to stop him."

There were murmurs of approval from around the room. A sincere and disinterested concern for the good of mankind was a much more morally justifiable reason for action than the protection of one's own selfish interest. Patinos, the man from Venezuela, looked at Benson with a smile of mild cynicism on his face. The smile signified nothing. Patinos, a sincere and devout Catholic, wore the same expression when he passed through the doors of his church.

"You seem very sure of this, Mr. Benson?"

"I've given quite some thought to it."

Borosoff said: "And just how do you propose to stop this madman, Mr. Benson?"

"I don't know."

"You don't know?" One of the others at the table lifted his eyebrows a millimeter—for him a sign of complete disapproval. "Then why did you summon us all this distance?"

"I didn't summon you. I asked you. I asked you to approve whatever course of action we might take."

"This course of action being—"

"Again, I don't know."

The eyebrows returned to normal. A twitch of the man's lip showed that he was contemplating smiling.

"This—ah—third party?"

"Yes."

"He has a name?"

"Cronkite. John Cronkite."

A hush descended upon the company. The

open objections had turned into pensive hesitation which in turn gave way to a nodding acceptance. Benson apart, no one there had ever met Cronkite, but his name was a household word to all of them. In the oil business that name had long been a legend, although at times a far from savory one. They all knew that any of them might require his incomparable services at any time, while at the same time hoping that that day would never come.

When it came to the capping of blazing gushers, Cronkite was without peer. Wherever in the world a gusher blew fire no one even considered putting it out themselves, they just sent for Cronkite. To wincing observers his *modus operandi* seemed nothing short of Draconian, but Cronkite would blasphemously brook no interference. Despite the extortionate fees he charged, it was more common than not for a four-engined jet to be put at his disposal to get him to the scene of the disaster as quickly as possible. Cronkite always delivered. He also knew all there was to know about the oil business. And he was, hardly surprisingly, extremely tough and utterly ruthless.

Henderson, who represented oil interests in Honduras, said: "Why should a man with his extraordinary qualifications, the world's number one, as we all know, choose to engage himself in—ah—an enterprise of this nature? From his reputation I would hardly have thought that he was one to be concerned about the woes of suffering mankind."

"He isn't. Money. Cronkite comes very high. A fresh challenge—the man's a born adventurer. But, basically, it's because he hates Lord Worth's guts."

Henderson said: "Not an uncommon sentiment, it seems. Why?"

"Lord Worth sent his own private Boeing for him to come cap a blazing gusher in the Middle East. By the time Cronkite arrived, Lord Worth's own men had capped it. This, alone, Cronkite regarded as a mortal insult. He then made the mistake of demanding the full fee for his services. Lord Worth has a reputation for notorious Scottish meanness, which, while an insult to the Scots, is more than justified in his case. He refused, and said that he would pay him for his time, no more. Cronkite then compounded his error by taking him to court. With the kind of lawyers Lord Worth can afford, Cronkite never had a chance. Not only did he lose but he had to pay the costs."

"Which wouldn't be low?" Henderson said.

"Medium-high to massive. I don't know. All I know is that Cronkite has done quite a bit of brooding about it ever since."

"Such a man would not have to be sworn to secrecy?"

"A man can swear a hundred different oaths and break them all. Besides, because of the exorbitant fees Cronkite charges, his feelings toward Lord Worth and the fact that he might just have to step outside the law, his silence is ensured."

It was the turn of another of those grouped round the table to raise his eyebrows. "Outside the law? We cannot risk being involved—"

" 'Might,' I said. For us, the element of risk does not exist."

"May we see this man?"

Benson nodded, rose, went to a door and admitted Cronkite.

Cronkite was a Texan. In height, build and cragginess of features he bore a remarkable resemblance to John Wayne. Unlike Wayne, he never smiled. His face was of a peculiarly yellow complexion, typical of those who have had an overdose of antimalarial tablets, which was just what had happened to Cronkite. Mepacrine does not make for a peaches-and-cream complexion— not that Cronkite's had ever remotely resembled that. He was newly returned from Indonesia, where he had inevitably maintained his 100 per cent record.

"Mr. Cronkite," Benson said. "Mr. Cronkite, this is—"

Cronkite was brusque. In a gravelly voice he said: "I don't want to know their names."

In spite of the abruptness of his tone, several of the oilmen round the table almost beamed.

Here was a man of discretion, a man after their own hearts.

Cronkite went on: "All I understand from Mr. Benson is that I am required to attend to a matter involving Lord Worth and the *Seawitch*. Mr. Benson has given me a pretty full briefing. I know the background. I would like, first of all, to hear any suggestions you gentlemen may have to offer." Cronkite sat down, lit what proved to be a very foul-smelling cigar, and waited expectantly.

He kept silent during the following half-hour discussion. For ten of the world's top businessmen, they proved to be an extraordinarily inept, not to say inane, lot. They talked in an ever-narrowing series of concentric circles.

Henderson said: "First of all, there must be no violence used. Is that agreed?"

Everybody nodded agreement. Each of them was a pillar of business respectability who could not afford to have his reputation besmirched in any way. No one appeared to notice that, except for lifting a hand to his cigar and puffing out increasingly vile clouds of smoke, Cronkite did not move throughout the discussion. He also remained totally silent.

After agreeing that there should be no violence, the meeting of ten agreed on nothing.

Finally Patinos spoke up. "Why don't you—one of you four Americans, I mean—approach your Congress to pass an emergency law banning offshore drilling in extraterritorial waters?"

Benson looked at him with something akin to pity. "I am afraid, sir, that you do not quite understand the relations between the American majors and Congress. On the few occasions we have met with them—something to do with too much profits and too little tax—I'm afraid we have treated them in so—ah—cavalier a fashion that nothing would give them greater pleasure than to refuse any request we might make."

One of the others, known simply as "Mr. A," said: "How about an approach to that international legal ombudsman, The Hague? After all, this is an international matter."

Henderson shook his head. "Forget it. The dilatoriness of that august body is so legendary that all present would be long retired—or worse—before a decision is made. The decision would just as likely be negative anyway."

"United Nations?" Mr. A said.

"That talk-shop!" Benson obviously had a low and not uncommon view of the UN. "They haven't even got the power to order New York to install a new parking meter outside their front door."

The next revolutionary idea came from one of the Americans.

"Why shouldn't we all agree, for an unspecified time—let's see how it goes—to *lower* our price below that of North Hudson? In that case no one would want to buy their oil."

This proposal was met with stunned disbelief.

Corral spoke in a kind voice. "Not only would that lead to vast losses to the major oil companies, but would almost certainly and immediately lead Lord Worth to lower *his* prices fractionally below their new ones. The man has sufficient working capital to keep him going for a hundred years at a loss—in the unlikely event, that is, of his running at a loss at all."

A lengthy silence followed. Cronkite was not quite as immobile as he had been. The granitic expression on his face remained unchanged, but the fingers of his nonsmoking hand had begun to drum gently on the armrest of his chair. For Cronkite, this was equivalent to throwing a fit of hysterics.

It was during this period that all thoughts of maintaining high, gentlemanly and ethical standards against drilling in international waters were forgotten by the ten.

"Why not," Mr. A said, "buy him out?" In fairness it has to be said that Mr. A did not appreciate just how wealthy Lord Worth was and that, immensely wealthy though he, Mr. A, was, Lord Worth could have bought *him* out lock, stock and barrel. "The *Seawitch* rights, I mean. A hundred million dollars. Let's be generous, two hundred million dollars. Why not?"

Corral looked depressed. "The answer to 'Why not?' is easy. By the latest reckoning, Lord Worth is one of the world's five richest men, and even two hundred million dollars would be pennies as far as he was concerned."

Now Mr. A looked depressed.

Benson said: "Sure he'd sell."

Mr. A visibly brightened.

"For two reasons only. In the first place he'd make a quick and splendid profit. In the second place, for less than half the selling price, he could build another *Seawitch*, anchor it a couple of miles away from the present *Seawitch*—there are no leasehold rights in extraterritorial waters— and start sending oil ashore at his same old price."

A temporarily deflated Mr. A slumped back in his armchair.

"A partnership, then," Mr. B said. His tone was that of a man in a state of quiet despair.

"Out of the question." Henderson was very positive. "Like all very rich men, Lord Worth is a born loner. He wouldn't have a combined partnership with the King of Saudi Arabia and the Shah of Iran, even if it were offered him free."

In the gloom of baffled and exhausted silence thoroughly bored and hitherto near-wordless, John Cronkite rose.

He said without preamble: "My personal fee will be one million dollars. I will require ten million dollars for operating expenses. Every cent of this will be accounted for and any un-spent balance returned. I demand a completely free hand and no interference from any of you. If I do encounter interference I'll retain the bal-ance of the expenses and abandon the mission. I refuse to disclose what my plans are—or will be when I have made them. Finally, I would prefer to have no further contact with any of you, now or at any time."

The assurance and confidence of the man were astonishing. Agreement among the mightily relieved ten was immediate and total. The ten million dollars—a trifling sum to those accus-tomed to spending as much in bribes every month or so—would be delivered within twenty-four—at the most, forty-eight—hours to a Cuban numbered account in Miami, the only place in the United States where Swiss-type numbered accounts were permitted. For tax-evasion pur-poses, the money of course would not come from any of their respective countries: instead, ironi-cally enough, from their bulging offshore funds.

Chapter 2

*L*ORD Worth was tall, lean and erect. His complexion was the mahogany hue of the playboy millionaire who spends his life in the sun: Lord Worth seldom worked less than sixteen hours a day. His abundant hair and mustache were snow-white. According to his mood and expression and to the eye of the beholder, he could have been a biblical patriarch, a better-class Roman senator, or a gentlemanly seventeenth-century pirate—except for the fact, of course, that none of those ever, far less habitually, wore lightweight Alpaca suits of the same color as Lord Worth's hair.

He looked and was every inch an aristocrat.
Unlike the many Americans who bore the Christian names of Duke or Earl, Lord Worth really
was a lord, the fifteenth in succession of a highly
distinguished family of Scottish peers of the
realm. The fact that their distinction had lain
mainly in the fields of assassination, endless clan
warfare, the stealing of women and cattle, and
the selling of their fellow peers down the river
was beside the point: the earlier Scottish peers
didn't go in too much for the more cultural
activities. The blue blood that had run in their
veins ran in Lord Worth's. As ruthless, preda-
tory, acquisitive and courageous as any of his
ancestors, Lord Worth simply went about his
business with a degree of refinement and so-
phistication that would have lain several light-
years beyond their understanding.

He had reversed the trend of Canadians
coming to Britain, making their fortunes and
eventually being elevated to the peerage: he
had already been a peer, and an extremely
wealthy one, before emigrating to Canada. His
emigration, which had been discreet and pre-
cipitous, had not been entirely voluntary. He
had made a fortune in real estate in London
before the Internal Revenue had become em-
barrassingly interested in his activities. Fortunately for him, whatever charges might have
been laid at his door were not extraditable.

He had spent several years in Canada, investing his millions in the North Hudson Oil Company and proving himself to be even more able in the oil business than he had been in real estate. His tankers and refineries spanned the globe before he had decided that the climate was too cold for him and moved south to Florida. His splendid mansion was the envy of the many millionaires—of a lesser financial breed, admittedly—who almost literally jostled for elbow-room in the Fort Lauderdale area.

The dining room in that mansion was something to behold. Monks, by the very nature of their calling, are supposed to be devoid of all earthly lusts, but no monk, past or present, could ever have gazed on the gleaming magnificence of that splendid oaken refectory table without turning pale chartreuse with envy. The chairs, inevitably, were Louis XIV. The splendidly embroidered silken carpet, with a pile deep enough for a fair-sized mouse to take cover in, would have been judged by an expert to come from Damascus and to have cost a fortune: the expert would have been right on both counts. The heavy drapes and embroidered silken walls were of the same pale gray, the latter being enhanced by a series of original impressionist paintings, no less than three by Matisse and the same number by Renoir. Lord Worth was no dilettante and was clearly trying to make amends for his ancestors' shortcomings in cultural fields.

It was in those suitably princely surroundings

that Lord Worth was at the moment taking his ease, reveling in his second brandy and the two beings whom—after money—he loved most in the world: his two daughters, Marina and Melinda, who had been so named by their now divorced Spanish mother. Both were young, both were beautiful, and could have been mistaken for twins, which they weren't: they were easily distinguishable by the fact that while Marina's hair was black as a raven's, Melinda's was pure titian.

There were two other guests at the table. Many a local millionaire would have given a fair slice of his ill-gotten gains for the privilege and honor of sitting at Lord Worth's table. Few were invited, and then but seldom. Those two young men, comparatively as poor as church mice, had the unique privilege, without invitation, of coming and going as they pleased, which was pretty often.

They were Mitchell and Roomer, two pleasant men in their early thirties for whom Lord Worth had a strong, if concealed, admiration and whom he held in something close to awe—inasmuch as they were the only two completely honest men he had ever met. Not that Lord Worth had ever stepped on the wrong side of the law, although he frequently had a clear view of what happened on the other side: it was simply that he was not in the habit of dealing with honest men. They had both been two highly efficient police sergeants, only they had been too efficient, much given to arresting the wrong people, such as crooked politicians and equally crooked wealthy businessmen who had previously labored under the misapprehension that they were above the law. They were fired, not to put too fine a point on it, for their total incorruptibility.

Of the two, Michael Mitchell was the taller, the broader and the less good-looking. With slightly craggy face, ruffled dark hair and blue chin, he could never have made it as a matinee idol. John Roomer, with his brown hair and trimmed brown mustache, was altogether better-looking. Both were shrewd, intelligent and highly experienced. Roomer was the intuitive one, Mitchell the one long on action. Apart from being charming, both men were astute and highly resourceful. And they were possessed of one other not inconsiderable quality: both were deadly marksmen.

Two years previously they had set up their own private investigative practice, and in that brief space of time had established such a repu-tation that people in real trouble now made a practice of going to them instead of to the police, a fact that hardly endeared them to the local law. They lived near Lord Worth's estate, where they were frequent and welcome visitors. That they did not come for the exclusive pleasure of his company Lord Worth was well aware. Nor, he knew, were they even in the slightest way in-terested in his money, a fact that Lord Worth found astonishing, as he had never previously encountered anyone who wasn't thus interested. What they were interested in, and deeply so, were Marina and Melinda.

The door opened and Lord Worth's butler, Jenkins—English, of course, as were the two footmen—made his usual soundless entrance, approached the head of the table and murmured discreetly in Lord Worth's ear. Lord Worth nodded and rose.

"Excuse me, girls, gentlemen. Visitors. I'm sure you can get along together quite well without me." He made his way to his study, entered and closed the door behind him—a very special padded door that, when shut, rendered the room completely soundproof.

The study, in its own way—Lord Worth was no sybarite but he liked his creature comforts as well as the next man—was as sumptuous as the dining room: oak, leather, a wholly unnecessary log fire burning in one corner, all straight from the best English baronial mansions. The walls were lined with thousands of books, many of which Lord Worth had actually read, a fact that must have caused great distress to his illiterate ancestors, who had despised degeneracy above all else.

A tall bronzed man with aquiline features and gray hair rose to his feet. Both men smiled and shook hands warmly.

Lord Worth said: "Corral, my dear chap! How

very nice to see you again. It's been quite some time."

"My pleasure, Lord Worth. Nothing recently that would have interested you."

"But now?"

"Now is something else again."

The Corral who stood before Lord Worth was indeed the Corral who, in his capacity as representative of the Florida offshore leases, had been present at the meeting of ten at Lake Tahoe. Some years had passed since he and Lord Worth had arrived at an amicable and mutually satisfactory agreement. Corral, widely regarded as Lord Worth's most avowedly determined enemy and certainly the most vociferous of his critics, reported regularly to Lord Worth on the current activities and, more importantly, the projected plans of the major companies, which didn't hurt Lord Worth at all. Corral, in return, received an annual tax-free retainer of $200,000, which didn't hurt him very much either.

Lord Worth pressed a bell and within seconds Jenkins entered bearing a silver tray with two large brandies. There was no telepathy involved, just years of experience and a long-established foreknowledge of Lord Worth's desires. When he left, both men sat.

Lord Worth said: "Well, what news from the West?"

"The Cherokee, I regret to say, are after you."

Lord Worth sighed and said: "It had to come sometime. Tell me all."

Corral told him all. He had a near-photographic memory and a gift for concise and accurate reportage. Within five minutes Lord Worth knew all that was worth knowing about the Lake Tahoe meeting.

Lord Worth who, because of the unfortunate misunderstanding that had arisen between himself and Cronkite, knew the latter as well as any and better than most, said at the end of Corral's report: "Did Cronkite subscribe to the ten's agreement to abjure any form of violence?"

"No."

"Not that it would have mattered if he had. Man's a total stranger to the truth. And ten million dollars' expenses, you tell me?"

"It did seem a bit excessive."

"Can you see a massive outlay like that being concomitant with anything except violence?"

"No."

"Do you think the others believed that there was no connection between them?"

"Let me put it this way, sir. Any group of people who can convince themselves, or appear to convince themselves, that any proposed action against you is for the betterment of mankind is also prepared to convince themselves, or appear to convince themselves, that the word 'Cronkite' is synonymous with peace on earth."

"So their consciences are clear. If Cronkite goes to any excessive lengths in death and destruction to achieve their ends, they can always throw up their hands in horror and say, 'Good God, we never thought the man would go that far.' Not that any connection between them and Cronkite would ever have to be established. What a bunch of devious, mealymouthed hypocrites!"

He paused for a moment.

"I suppose Cronkite refused to divulge his plans?"

"Absolutely. But there is one odd circumstance: just as we were leaving, Cronkite drew two of the ten to one side and spoke to them privately. It would be interesting to know why."

"Any chance of finding out?"

"A fair chance. Nothing guaranteed. But I'm sure Benson could find out—after all, it was Benson who invited us all to Lake Tahoe."

"And you think you could persuade Benson to tell you?"

"A fair chance. Nothing more."

Lord Worth put on his resigned expression. "All right, how much?"

"Nothing. Money won't buy Benson." Corral shook his head in disbelief. "Extraordinary, in this day and age, but Benson is not a mercenary man. But he does owe me some favors, one of them being that, without me, he wouldn't be the president of the oil company that he is now." Corral paused. "I'm surprised you haven't asked me the identities of the two men Cronkite took aside."

"So am I."

"Borosoff of the Soviet Union and Patinos of Venezuela." Lord Worth appeared to lapse into a trance. "That mean anything to you?"

Lord Worth bestirred himself. "Yes. Units of the Russian Navy are making a so-called 'goodwill tour' of the Caribbean. They are, inevitably, based in Cuba. Of the ten, those are the only two that could bring swift—ah—naval intervention to bear against the *Seawitch*." He shook his head. "Diabolical. Utterly diabolical."

"My way of thinking too, sir. There's no knowing. But I'll check as soon as possible and hope to get results."

"And I shall take immediate precautions." Both men rose. "Corral, we shall have to give serious consideration to the question of increasing this paltry retainer of yours."

"We try to be of service, Lord Worth."

Lord Worth's private radio room bore more than a passing resemblance to the flight deck of his private 707. The variety of knobs, switches, buttons and dials was bewildering. Lord Worth seemed perfectly at home with them all, and proceeded to make a number of calls.

The first were to his four helicopter pilots, instructing them to have his two largest helicopters—never a man to do things by halves,

Lord Worth owned no fewer than six of these machines—ready at his own private airfield shortly before dawn. The next four were to people of whose existence his fellow directors were totally unaware. The first of these calls was to Cuba, the second to Venezuela. Lord Worth's worldwide range of contacts—employees, rather—was vast. The instructions to both were simple and explicit. A constant monitoring watch was to be kept on the naval bases in both countries, and any sudden departures of any naval vessels, and their type, was to be reported to him immediately.

The third, to a person who lived not too many miles away, was addressed to a certain Giuseppe Palermo, whose name sounded as if he might be a member of the Mafia, but who definitely wasn't: the Mafia Palermo despised as a molly-coddling organization which had become so ludicrously gentle in its methods of persuasion as to be in imminent danger of becoming respectable. The next call was to Baton Rouge in Louisiana, where lived a person who called himself only "Conde" and whose main claim to fame lay in the fact that he was the highest-ranking naval officer to have been court-martialed and dishonorably discharged since World War II. He, like the others, received very explicit instructions. Not only was Lord Worth a master organizer, but the efficiency he displayed was matched only by his speed in operation.

The noble Lord, who would have stoutly maintained—if anyone had the temerity to accuse him, which no one ever had—that he was no criminal, was about to become just that. Even this he would have strongly denied, and that on three grounds. The Constitution upheld the right of every citizen to bear arms; every man had the right to defend himself and his property against criminal attack by whatever means lay to hand; and the only way to fight fire was with fire.

The final call Lord Worth put through, and this time with total confidence, was to his tried and trusted lieutenant, Commander Larsen.

Commander Larsen was the captain of the *Seawitch.*

Larsen—no one knew why he called himself "Commander," and he wasn't the kind of person you asked—was a rather different breed of man from his employer. Except in a public court or in the presence of a law officer, he would cheerfully admit to anyone that he was both a non-gentleman *and* a criminal. And he certainly bore no resemblance to any aristocrat, alive or dead. But there did exist a genuine rapport and mutual respect between Lord Worth and himself. In all likelihood they were simply brothers under the skin.

As a criminal and non-aristocrat—and casting no aspersions on honest unfortunates who may resemble him—he certainly looked the part. He had the general build and appearance of the more viciously daunting heavyweight wrestler, deep-set black eyes that peered out under the overhanging foliage of hugely bushy eyebrows, an equally bushy black beard, a hooked nose, and a face that looked as if it had been in regular contact with a series of heavy objects. No one, with the possible exception of Lord Worth, knew who he was, what he had been, or from where he had come. His voice, when he spoke, came as a positive shock: beneath that Neanderthalic façade was the voice and the mind of an educated man. It really ought not to have come as such a shock: beneath the façade of many an exquisite fop lies the mind of a retarded fourth-grader.

Larsen was in the radio room at that moment, listening attentively, nodding from time to time; then he flicked a switch that put the incoming call on the loudspeaker.

He said: "All clear, sir. Everything understood. We'll make the preparations. But haven't you overlooked something, sir?"

"Overlooked what?" Lord Worth's voice over the telephone carried the overtones of a man who couldn't possibly have overlooked anything.

"You've suggested that armed surface vessels may be used against us. If they're prepared to go to such lengths, isn't it feasible that they'll go to *any* lengths?"

"Get to the point, man."

"The point is that it's easy enough to keep an

eye on a couple of naval bases. But I suggest it's a bit more difficult to keep an eye on a dozen, maybe two dozen, airfields."

"Good God!" There was a long pause during which the rattle of cogs and the meshing of gear wheels in Lord Worth's brain couldn't be heard. "Do you really think—"

"If I were the *Seawitch,* Lord Worth, it would be six and half-a-dozen to me whether I was clobbered by shells or bombs. And planes could get away from the scene of the crime a damn sight faster than ships. They could get clean away, whereas the U. S. Navy or land-based bombers would have a good chance of intercepting surface vessels. And another thing, Lord Worth—a ship could stop at a distance of a hundred miles. No distance at all for the guided missile: I believe they have a range of four thousand miles these days. When the missile was, say, twenty miles from us, they could switch on its heat-source tracking device. God knows, we're the only heat source for a hundred miles around."

Another lengthy pause, then: "Any more encouraging thoughts occur to you, Commander Larsen?"

"Yes, sir. Just one. If I were the enemy—I may call them the enemy—"

"Call the devils what you want."

"If I were the enemy I'd use a submarine. They don't even have to break the surface to loose off a missile. Poof! No *Seawitch.* No signs of any attacker. Could well be put down to a massive explosion aboard the *Seawitch*. Far from impossible, sir."

"You'll be telling me next that they'll be atomic-headed missiles."

"To be picked up by a dozen seismological stations? I should think it hardly likely, sir. But that may just be wishful thinking. I, personally, have no wish to be vaporized."

"I'll see you in the morning." The speaker went dead.

Larsen hung up his phone and smiled widely. One might have expected this action to reveal a set of yellowed fangs: instead, it revealed a perfect set of gleamingly white teeth. He turned to look at Scoffield, his head driller and right-hand man.

Scoffield was a large, rubicund, smiling man, apparently the easygoing essence of good nature. To the fact that this was not precisely the case, any member of his drilling crews would have eagerly and blasphemously testified. Scoffield was a very tough citizen indeed, and one could assume that it was not innate modesty that made him conceal the fact: much more probably it was a permanent stricture of the facial muscles caused by the four long vertical scars on his cheeks, two on either side. Clearly he, like Larsen, was no great advocate of plastic surgery. He looked at Larsen with understandable curiosity.

"What was all that about?"

"The day of reckoning is at hand. Prepare to meet thy doom. More specifically, his lordship is beset by enemies." Larsen outlined Lord Worth's plight. "He's sending what sounds like a battalion of hard men out here in the early morning, accompanied by suitable weaponry. Then in the afternoon we are to expect a boat of some sort, loaded with even heavier weaponry."

"I wonder where he's getting all those hard men and weaponry from."

"One wonders. One does not ask."

"All this talk—your talk—about bombers and submarines and missiles. Do you believe that?"

"No. It's just that it's hard to pass up the opportunity to ruffle the aristocratic plumage." He paused, then said thoughtfully: "At least I hope I don't believe it. Come on, let us examine our defenses."

"You've got a pistol. I've got a pistol. That's defenses?"

"Well, where we'll mount the defenses when they arrive. Fixed large-bore guns, I should imagine."

"*If* they arrive."

"Give the devil his due. Lord Worth delivers."

"From his own private armory, I suppose."

"It wouldn't surprise me."

"What do you really think, Commander?"

"I don't know. All I know is that if Lord

Worth is even halfway right, life aboard may become slightly less monotonous in the next few days."

The two men moved out into the gathering dusk on the platform. The *Seawitch* was moored in a hundred and fifty fathoms of water—nine hundred feet, which was well within the tensioning cables' capacities—safely south of the U.S. mineral leasing blocks and the great east-west fairway, right on top of the biggest oil reservoir yet discovered around the shores of the Gulf of Mexico. The two men paused at the drilling derrick where a drill, at its maximum angled capacity, was trying to determine the extent of the oilfield. The crew looked at them without any particular affection but not with hostility. There was reason for the lack of warmth.

Before any laws were passed making such drilling illegal, Lord Worth wanted to scrape the bottom of this gigantic barrel of oil. Not that he was particularly worried, for government agencies are notoriously slow to act: but there was always the possibility that they might bestir themselves this time and that, horror of horrors, the bonanza might turn out to be vastly larger than estimated.

Hence the present attempt to discover the limits of the strike and hence the lack of warmth. Hence the reason why Larsen and Scoffield, both highly gifted slave drivers, born centuries out of their time, drove their men day and night. The men disliked it, but not to the point of rebellion. They were highly paid, well-housed and well-fed. True, there was little enough in the way of wine, women and song, but then, after an exhausting twelve-hour shift, those frivolities couldn't hope to compete with the attractions of a massive meal, then a long, deep sleep. More importantly and most unusually, the men were paid a bonus on every thousand barrels of oil.

Larsen and Scoffield made their way to the western apex of the platform and gazed out at the massive bulk of the storage tank, its topsides festooned with warning lights. They gazed at this for some time, then turned and walked back toward the accommodation quarters.

Scoffield said: "Decided on your gun emplacements yet, Commander—if there are any guns?"

"There'll be guns." Larsen was confident. "But we won't need any in this quarter."

"Why?"

"Work it out for yourself. As for the rest, I'm not too sure. It'll come to me in my sleep. My turn for an early night. See you at four."

The oil was not stored aboard the rig—it is forbidden by a law based strictly on common sense to store hydrocarbons at or near the working platform of an oil rig. Instead, Lord Worth, on Larsen's instructions—which had prudently come in the form of suggestions—had had built a huge floating tank which was anchored, on a basis precisely similar to that of the *Seawitch* herself, at a distance of about three hundred yards. Cleaned oil was pumped into this after it came up from the ocean floor, or, more precisely, from a massive limestone reef deep down below the ocean floor, a reef caused by tiny marine creatures of a now long-covered shallow sea of some half a billion years ago.

Once, sometimes twice, a day a 50,000-ton-capacity tanker would stop by and empty the huge tank. There were three of those tankers employed on the crisscross run to the southern United States. The North Hudson Oil Company did, in fact, have supertankers, but the use of them in this case did not serve Lord Worth's purpose. Even the entire contents of the *Sea-witch*'s tank would not have filled a quarter of the supertanker's carrying capacity, and the possibility of a supertanker running at a loss, however small, would have been the source of waking nightmares for the North Hudson: equally importantly, the more isolated ports which Lord Worth favored for the delivery of his oil were unable to offer deep-water berthside facilities for anything in excess of fifty thousand tons.

It might be explained, in passing, that Lord Worth's choice of those obscure ports was not entirely fortuitous. Among the parties to the gentlemen's agreement against offshore drilling, some of the most vociferous of those who roundly condemned North Hudson's nefarious practices were, regrettably, North Hudson's best customers. They were the smaller companies who operated on marginal profits and lacked the resources to engage in research and exploration, which the larger companies did, investing allegedly vast sums in those projects and then, to the continuous fury of the Internal Revenue Service and the anger of numerous Congressional investigation committees, claiming even vaster tax exemptions.

But to the smaller companies the lure of cheaper oil was irresistible. The *Seawitch*, which probably produced as much oil as all the government official leasing areas combined, seemed a sure and perpetual source of cheap oil—at least until the government stepped in, which might or might not happen in the next decade: the big companies had already demonstrated their capacity to deal with inept Congressional inquiries, and as long as the energy crisis continued nobody was going to worry very much about where oil came from, as long as it came. In addition, the smaller companies felt, if the OPEC—the Organization of Petroleum Exporting Countries— could play ducks and drakes with oil prices whenever they felt like it, why couldn't they?

Less than two miles from Lord Worth's estate were the adjacent homes and combined office of Michael Mitchell and John Roomer. It was Mitchell who answered the doorbell.

The visitor was of medium height, slightly tubby, wore wire-rimmed glasses, and alopecia had hit him hard. He said: "May I come in?" in a clipped but courteous enough voice.

"Sure." Michael Mitchell let him in to their apartment. "We don't usually see people this late."

"Thank you. I come on unusual business. James Bentley." A little sleight of hand and a card appeared. "FBI."

Mitchell didn't even look at it. "You can have those things made at any joke shop. Where you from?"

"Miami."

"Phone number?"

Bentley reversed the card, which Mitchell handed to Roomer. "My memory man. Saves me from having to have a memory of my own."

Roomer didn't glance at the card either. "It's okay, Mike. I have him. You're the boss man up there, aren't you?" A nod. "Please sit down, Mr. Bentley."

"One thing clear, first," Mitchell said. "Are *we* under investigation?"

"On the contrary. The State Department has asked us to ask you to help them."

"Status at last," Mitchell said. "We've got it made, John—except for one thing: the State Department doesn't know who the hell we are."

"*I* do." Discussion closed. "I understand you gentlemen are friendly with Lord Worth."

Roomer was careful. "We know him slightly, socially—just as you seem to know a little about us."

"I know a lot about you, including the fact that you are a couple of ex-cops who never learned to look the right way at the right time and the wrong way at the wrong time. Bars the ladder to promotion. I want you to carry out a little investigation of Lord Worth."

"No deal," Mitchell said. "We know him slightly better than slightly."

"Hear him out, Mike." But Roomer's face, too, had lost whatever little friendliness it may have held.

"Lord Worth has been making loud noises— over the phone—to the State Department. He seems to be suffering from a persecution complex. This interests the State Department, because they see him more in the role of the persecutor than persecuted."

"You mean the FBI does," Roomer said. "You've had him in your files for years. Lord Worth always gives the impression of being very capable of looking out for himself."

"That's precisely what intrigues the State Department."

Mitchell said: "What kind of noises?"

"Nonsense noises. You know he has an oil rig out in the Gulf of Mexico?"

"The *Seawitch?* Yes."

"He appears to be under the impression that

the *Seawitch* is in mortal danger. He wants protection. Very modest in his demands, as becomes a multimillionaire—a missile frigate or two, some missile fighters standing by, just in case."

"In case of what?"

"That's the question. He refused to say. Just said he had secret information—which, in fact, wouldn't surprise me. The Lord Worths of this world have their secret agents everywhere."

"You'd better level with us," Mitchell said.

"I've told you all I know. The rest is surmise. Calling the State Department means that there are foreign countries involved. There are Soviet naval vessels in the Caribbean at present. The State Department smells an international incident or worse."

"What do you want us to do?"

"Not much. Just to find out Lord Worth's intended movements for the next day or two."

Mitchell said: "And if we refuse? We have our licenses rescinded?"

"I am not a corrupt police chief. If you refuse, you can just forget that you ever saw me. But I thought you might care enough about Lord Worth to help protect him against himself or the consequences of any rash action he might take. I thought you might care even more about the reactions of his two daughters if anything were to happen to their father."

Mitchell stood up, jerked a thumb. "The door. You know too damn much."

"Sit down." A sudden-chill asperity. "Don't be foolish: it's my job to know too damn much. But apart from Lord Worth and his family, I thought you might have some little concern for your country's welfare."

Roomer said: "Isn't that pitching it a little high?"

"Very possibly. But it is the policy of the State Department, the Justice Department and the FBI not to take any chances."

Roomer said: "You're putting us in a damned awkward situation."

"Don't think I don't appreciate that. I know I've put you on a spot and I'm sorry, but I'm afraid you'll have to resolve that particular dilemma yourselves."

Mitchell said: "Thanks for dropping this little problem in our laps. What do you expect us to do? Go to Lord Worth, ask him why he's been hollering to the State Department, ask him what he's up to and what his immediate plans are?"

Bentley smiled. "Nothing so crude. You have a reputation—except, of course, in the police department—of being, in the street phrase, a couple of slick operators. The approach is up to you." He stood. "Keep that card and let me know when you find out anything. How long would that take, do you think?"

Roomer said: "A couple of hours."

"A couple of hours?" Even Bentley seemed

momentarily taken aback. "You don't, then, re-quire an invitation to visit the baronial mansion?"

"No."

"Millionaires do."

"We aren't even thousandaires."

"It makes a difference. Well, thank you very much, gentlemen. Goodnight."

After Bentley's departure the two men sat for a couple of minutes in silence, then Mitchell said: "We play it both ways?"

"We play it every way." Roomer reached for a phone, dialed a number and asked for Lord Worth. He had to identify himself before he was put through—Lord Worth was a man who re-spected his privacy.

Roomer said: "Lord Worth? Roomer. Mitchell and I have something to discuss with you, sir, which may or may not be of urgency and im-portance. We would prefer not to discuss it over the phone." He paused, listened for a few moments, murmured a thank you and hung up.

"He'll see us right away. Says to park the car in the lane. Side door. Study. Says the girls have gone upstairs."

"Think our friend Bentley already has our phone tapped?"

"Not worth his FBI salt if he hasn't."

Five minutes later, car parked in the lane, they were making their way through the trees to the side door. Their progress was observed with interest by Marina, standing by the window in her upstairs bedroom. She looked thoughtful for a moment, then turned and unhurriedly left the room.

Lord Worth welcomed the two men in his study and securely closed the padded door behind them. He swung open the doors of a concealed bar and poured three brandies. There were times when one rang for Jenkins and there were times when one didn't. He lifted his glass.

"Health. An unexpected pleasure."

"It's no pleasure for us," Roomer said gloomily.

"Then you haven't come to ask me for my daughters' hands in marriage?"

"No, sir," Mitchell said. "No such luck. John here is better at explaining these things."

"What things?"

"We've just had a visit from a senior FBI agent." Roomer handed over Bentley's card. "There's a number on the back that we're to ring when we've extracted some information from you."

"How very interesting." There was a long pause, then Lord Worth looked at each man in turn. "What kind of information?"

"In Bentley's words, you have been making 'loud noises' to the State Department. According to them, you seem to think that the *Seawitch* is under threat. They want to know where you got this secret information, and what your proposed movements are."

"Why didn't the FBI come directly to me?"

"Because you wouldn't have told them any more than you told the State Department. If, that is to say, you'd even let them over the threshold of your house. But they know—Bentley told us this—that we come across here now and again, so I suppose they figured you'd be less off your guard with us."

"So Bentley figures that you'd craftily wring some careless talk from me without my being aware that I was talking carelessly."

"Something like that."

"But doesn't this put you in a somewhat invidious position?"

"Not really."

"But you're supposed to uphold the law, no?"

"Yes." Mitchell spoke with some feeling. "But not organized law. Or have you forgotten, Lord Worth, that we're a couple of ex-cops because we wouldn't go along with your so-called organized law? Our only responsibility is to our clients."

"I'm not your client."

"No."

"Would you like me to be your client?"

Roomer said: "What on earth for?"

"It's never something for nothing in this world, John. Services have to be rewarded."

"Failure of a mission." Mitchell was on his feet. "Nice of you to see us, Lord Worth."

"I apologize." Lord Worth sounded genuinely contrite. "I'm afraid I rather stepped out of line there." He paused ruminatively, then smiled. "Just trying to recall when last I apologized to anybody. I seem to have a short memory. Bless my lovely daughters. Information for our friends of the FBI? First, I received my information in context of several anonymous threats—telephone calls—on the lives of my daughters. A double-barreled threat, if you will, against the girls if I didn't stop the flow of oil. As they pointed out, I can't hide them forever and there's nothing one can do against a sniper's bullet—and if I were too difficult they'd have the *Seawitch* blown out of the water. As for my future movements, I'm going out to the *Seawitch* tomorrow afternoon and will remain there for twenty-four hours, perhaps forty-eight."

Roomer said: "Any truth in either of those two statements?"

"Don't be preposterous. Of course not. I *am* going out to the rig—but before dawn. I don't want those beady-eyed bandits watching me from the undergrowth at my heliport as I take off."

"You are referring to the FBI, sir?"

"Who else? Will that do for the moment?"

"Splendidly."

They walked back to the lane in silence.

Roomer got in behind the wheel of the car, Mitchell beside him.

Roomer said: "Well, well, well."

"Well, as you say, well, well, well. Crafty old devil."

Marina's voice came from the back. "Crafty he may be, but—"

She broke off in a gasp as Mitchell whirled in his seat and Roomer switched on his interior lights. The barrel of Mitchell's .38 was lined up between her eyes, eyes at the moment wide with shock and fear.

Mitchell said in a soft voice: "Don't ever do that to me again. Next time it may be too late."

She licked her lips. She was normally as high-spirited and independent as she was beautiful, but it is a rather disconcerting thing to look down the muzzle of a pistol for the first time in your life. "I was just going to say that he may be crafty but he's neither old nor a devil. Will you please put that gun away? You don't point guns at people you love."

Mitchell's gun disappeared. He said: "You shouldn't fall in love with crazy young fools."

"Or spies." Roomer was looking at Melinda. "What are you two doing here?"

Melinda was more composed than her sister. After all, she hadn't had to look down the barrel of a pistol. She said: "And you, John Roomer, are a crafty young devil. You're just stalling for time." Which was quite true.

"What's that supposed to mean?"

"It means you're thinking furiously of the answer to the same question we're about to ask you. What are *you* two doing here?"

"That's none of your business." Roomer's normally soft-spoken voice was unaccustomedly and deliberately harsh.

There was a silence from the back seat, both girls realizing that there was more to the men than they had thought, and the gap between their social and professional lives wider than they had thought.

Mitchell sighed. "Let's cool it, John. An ungrateful child is sharper than a serpent's tooth."

"Jesus!" Roomer shook his head. "You can say that again." He hadn't the faintest idea what Mitchell was talking about.

Mitchell said: "Why don't you go to your father and ask him? I'm sure he'll tell you—along with the roughest chewing-out you've ever had for interfering in his private business." He got out, opened the rear door, waited until the sisters got out, closed the rear door, said 'Goodnight' and returned to his seat, leaving the girls standing uncertainly at the side of the road.

Roomer drove off. He said: "Very masterful, though I didn't like our doing it. God knows, they meant no harm. In any case, it may stand us in good stead in the future."

"It'll stand us in even better stead if we get

to the phone booth right around the corner as soon as we can."

They reached the booth in fifteen seconds, and one minute later Mitchell emerged from it. As he took his seat Roomer said: "What was all that about?"

"Sorry, private matter." Mitchell handed Roomer a piece of paper. Roomer switched on the overhead light. On the paper Mitchell had scrawled: "This car bugged?"

Roomer said: "Okay by me." They drove home in silence. Standing in his carport Roomer said: "What makes you think my car's bugged?"

"Nothing. How far do you trust Bentley?"

"You know how far. But he—or one of his men—wouldn't have had time."

"Five seconds isn't a long time. That's all the time it takes to attach a magnetic clamp."

They searched the car, then Mitchell's. Both were clean. In Mitchell's kitchen Roomer said: "Your phone call?"

"The old boy, of course. I got to him before the girls did. Told him what had happened and that he was to tell them he'd received threats against their lives, that he knew the source, that he didn't trust the local law and so had sent for us to deal with the matter. Caught on at once. Also to give them hell for interfering."

Roomer said: "He'll convince them."

"More importantly, did he convince you?"

"No. He thinks fast on his feet and lies even

faster. He wanted to find out how seriously he would be taken in the case of a real emergency. He now has the preliminary evidence that he is being taken seriously. You have to hand it to him—as devious as they come. I suppose we tell Bentley exactly what he told us to tell him?"

"What else?"

"Do you believe what he told us?"

"That he has his own private intelligence corps? I wouldn't question it for a moment. That he's going out to the *Seawitch?* I believe that, too. I'm not so sure about his timing, though. We're to tell Bentley that he's leaving in the afternoon. He told us he's leaving about dawn. If he can lie to Bentley he can lie to us. I don't know why he should think it necessary to lie to us, probably just his second nature. I think he's going to leave much sooner than that."

Roomer said: "Me, too, I'm afraid. If I intended to be up at dawn's early light I'd be in bed by now or heading that way. He showed no sign of going to bed, so I conclude he has no intention of going to bed, because it wouldn't be worth his while." He paused. "So. A double stake-out?"

"I thought so. Up by Lord Worth's house and down by his heliport. You for the heliport, me for the tail job?"

"What else?" Mitchell was possessed of phenomenal night-sight. Except on the very blackest of nights he could drive without any lights at all.

"I'll hole up behind the west spinney. You know it?"

"I know it. How about you feeding the story to Bentley while I make a couple of thermoses of coffee and some sandwiches?"

"Fine." Roomer reached for the phone, then paused. "Listen, why are we doing all this? We don't owe the FBI anything. We have no authority from anyone to do anything. You said it yourself: we and organized law walk in different directions. I don't feel I'm under any obligation to save my country from a nonexistent threat. We've got no client, no commission, no prospect of fees. Why should we care if Lord Worth sticks his head into a noose?"

Mitchell paused in slicing bread. "As far as your last question is concerned, why don't you call up Melinda and ask her?"

Roomer gave him a long, quizzical look, sighed and reached for the telephone.

Chapter 3

SCOFFIELD had been wrong in his guess. Lord Worth was possessed of no private arsenal. But the United States armed services were, and in their dozens, at that.

The two break-ins were accomplished with the professional expertise born of a long and arduous practice that precluded any possibility of mistakes. The targets in both cases were government arsenals, one army and one naval. Both, naturally, were manned by round-the-clock guards, none of whom was killed or even injured if one were to disregard the cranial contusions—and those were few—caused by sandbagging and sapping: Lord Worth had been very explicit on the use of minimal violence.

Giuseppe Palermo, who looked and dressed like a successful Wall Street broker, had the more difficult task of the two, although, as a man who held the Mafia in tolerant contempt, he regarded the exercise as almost childishly easy. Accompanied by nine almost equally respectable men—sartorially respectable, that is—three of whom were dressed as army majors, he arrived at the Florida arms depot at fifteen minutes to midnight. The six young guards, none of whom had even seen or heard a shot fired in anger, were at their drowsiest and expecting nothing but their midnight reliefs. Only two were really fully awake—the other four had dozed away—and those two, responding to a heavy and peremptory hammering on the main entrance door, were disturbed, not to say highly alarmed, by the appearance of three army officers who announced that they were making a snap inspection to test security and alertness. Five minutes later all six were bound and gagged—two of them unconcious and due to wake up with very sore heads because of their misguided attempts to put up a show of resistance—and safely locked up in one of the many so-called secure rooms in the depot.

During this period and the next twenty minutes, one of Palermo's men, an electronics expert called Jamieson, made a thorough search for all the external alarm signals to both the police and nearest military HQ. He either bypassed or disconnected them all.

It was when he was engaged in this that the relief guards, almost as drowsy as those whom they had been expecting to find, made their appearance and were highly disconcerted to find themselves looking at the muzzles of three machine carbines. Within minutes, securely bound but not gagged, they had joined the previous guards, whose gags were now removed. They could now shout until doomsday, as the nearest habitation was more than a mile away: the temporary gagging of the first six guards had been merely for the purpose of preventing their warning off their reliefs.

Palermo now had almost eight hours before the break-in could be discovered.

He sent one of his men, Watkins, to bring round to the front the concealed minibus in which they had arrived. All of them, Watkins excepted, changed from their conservative clothing and military uniforms into rough workclothes, which resulted in rather remarkable changes in their appearance and character. While they were doing this, Watkins went to the depot garage, picked a surprisingly ineffectual lock, selected a two-ton truck, hot-wired the ignition—the keys were, understandably, missing—and drove out to the already open main loading doors of the depot.

Palermo had brought along with him one by

the name of Jacobson who, between sojourns in various penitentiaries, had developed to a remarkable degree the fine art of opening any type of lock, combination or otherwise. Fortunately his services were not needed, for nobody, curiously enough, had taken the trouble to conceal some score of keys hanging on the wall in the main office.

In less than half an hour Palermo and his men had loaded aboard the truck—chosen because it was a covered-van type—a staggering variety of weaponry, ranging from bazookas to machine pistols, together with sufficient ammunition for a battalion and a considerable amount of high explosives. Then they relocked the doors and took the keys with them—when the next relief arrived at eight in the morning it would take them that much longer to discover what had actually happened. After that, they locked the loading and main entrance doors.

Watkins drove the minibus, with its load of discarded clothes, back to its place of concealment, returned to the truck and drove off. The other nine sat or lay in varying degrees of discomfort among the weaponry in the back. It was as well for them that it was only twenty minutes' drive to Lord Worth's private, isolated and deserted heliport—deserted, that is, except for two helicopters, their pilots and copilots.

The truck, using only its sidelights, came

through the gates of the heliport and drew up alongside one of the helicopters. Discreet portable loading lights were switched on, casting hardly more than a dull glow, but sufficient for a man only eighty yards away and equipped with a pair of night glasses to distinguish clearly what was going on. And Roomer, prone in the spinney with the binoculars to his eyes, was only eighty yards away. No attempt had been made to wrap or in any way to disguise the nature of the cargo. It took only twenty minutes to unload the truck and stow its contents away in the helicopter under the watchful eye of a pilot with a keen regard for weight distribution.

Palermo and his men, with the exception of Watkins, boarded the other helicopter and sat back to await promised reinforcements. The pilot of this helicopter had already, as was customary, radio-filed his flight plan to the nearest airport, accurately giving his destination as the *Seawitch*. To have done otherwise would have been foolish indeed. The radar tracking systems along the Gulf states are as efficient as any in the world, and any course deviation from a falsely declared destination would have meant that, in very short order, two highly suspicious pilots in supersonic jets would be flying alongside and asking some very unpleasant questions.

Watkins drove the truck back to the garage,

dewired the ignition, locked the door, retrieved the minibus and left. Before dawn, all his friends' clothes would have been returned to their apartments, and the minibus, which had of course been stolen, to its parking lot.

Roomer was getting bored and his elbows were becoming sore. Since the minibus had driven away some half hour ago he had remained in the same prone position, his night glasses seldom far from his eyes. His sandwiches were gone, as was all his coffee, and he would have given much for a cigarette but decided it would be unwise. Clearly those aboard the helicopters were waiting for something, and that something could only be the arrival of Lord Worth.

He heard the sound of an approaching engine and saw another vehicle, with only sidelights on, turn through the gateway. It was another minibus. Whoever was inside was not the man he was waiting for, he knew: Lord Worth was not much given to traveling in minibuses. The vehicle drew up alongside the passenger helicopter and its passengers disembarked and climbed aboard the helicopter. Roomer counted twelve in all.

The last was just disappearing inside the helicopter when another vehicle arrived. This one didn't pass through the gateway; it swept through it, with only parking lights on. A Rolls Royce. Lord Worth, for a certainty. As if to redouble his certainty, there came to his ears the soft swish of tires on the grass. He twisted round to see a car, both lights and engine off, coasting to a soundless stop beside his own.

"Over here," Roomer called softly. Mitchell joined him, and together they watched the white-clad figure of Lord Worth leave the Rolls and mount the steps to the helicopter. "I guess that completes the payload for the night."

"The payload being?"

"There are twenty-one other passengers aboard that machine. I can't swear to it, but instinct tells me they are not honest, upright citizens. They say that every multimillionaire has his own private army. I think I've just seen one of Lord Worth's platoons filing by."

"The second chopper's not involved?"

"It sure is. It's the star of the show—loaded to the gunwales with armament."

"That's not a crime in itself. Could be part of Lord Worth's private collection. He's got one of the biggest in the country."

"Private citizens aren't allowed to have bazookas, machine guns and high explosives in their collections."

"He borrowed them, you think?"

"Yeah. Without payment or receipt."

"The nearest government arsenal?"

"I'd say so."

"They're still sitting there. Maybe they're waiting a preset time before takeoff. Might be some time. Let's go to one of the cars and radio the law."

"The nearest army command post is seven miles from here."

"Right."

The two men were on their feet and had taken only two steps toward the cars when, almost simultaneously, the engines of both helicopters started up with their usual clattering roar. Seconds later both machines lifted off.

Mitchell said: "Well, it was a thought."

" 'Was' is right. Look at 'em go: honest God-fearing citizens with all their navigational lights on."

"That's in case someone bumps into them," Mitchell said. "We could call up the nearest air force base and have them forced down."

"On what grounds?"

"Stolen government property."

"No evidence. Just our say-so. They'll find out Lord Worth is aboard. Who's going to take the word of a couple of busted cops against his?"

"No one. A sobering thought. Ever felt like a pariah?"

"Like now. I feel goddamned helpless. Well, let's go and find some evidence. Where's the nearest arsenal from here?"

"About a mile from the command post. I know where."

"Why don't they keep their damned arsenals *inside* the command posts?"

"Because ammunition can and does blow up. How would you like to be sitting in a crowded barracks when an ammo dump blew up next door?"

Roomer straightened from the keyhole of the main door of the arms depot and reluctantly pocketed the very large set of keys which any ill-disposed law officer could have jailed him for carrying.

"I thought I could open any door with this bunch. But not this one. Give you one guess where the keys are now."

"Probably sailing down from a chopper into the Gulf."

"Right. Those loading doors have the same lock. Besides that, nothing but barred windows. You don't have a hacksaw on you, do you, Mike?"

"I will next time." He shone his flashlight through one of the barred windows. All he could see was his own reflection. He took out his pistol and, holding it by the barrel, struck the heavy butt several times against the glass, without any noticeable effect—hardly surprising, considering that the window lay several inches beyond the bars and the force of the blows was minimal.

Roomer said: "What are you trying to do?"

Mitchell was patient. "Break the glass."

"Breaking the glass won't help you get inside."

"It'll help me see and maybe hear. I wonder if that's just plate glass or armored stuff."

"How should I know?"

"Well, we'll find out. If it's armored, the bullet will ricochet. Get down." Both men crouched and Mitchell fired one shot at an upward angle. The bullet did not ricochet. It passed through, leaving a jagged hole with radiating cracks. Mitchell began chipping away round the hole but desisted when Roomer appeared with a heavy car jack-handle: a few powerful blows and Roomer had a hole almost a foot in diameter. Mitchell shone his flash through this: an office lined with filing cabinets and an open door beyond. He put his ear as close to the hole as possible and he heard it at once, the faint but unmistakable sound of metal clanging against metal and the shouting of unmistakably hoarse voices. Mitchell withdrew his head and nodded to Roomer, who leaned forward and listened in turn.

Roomer straightened and said: "There are a lot of frustrated people in there."

About a mile beyond the entrance to the army command post they stopped by a roadside telephone booth. Mitchell telephoned the army post, told them the state of defenses at their arsenal building would bear investigation and that it would be advisable for them to bring along a duplicate set of keys for the main door. When asked who was speaking he hung up and returned to Roomer's car.

"Too late to call in the Air Force now, I suppose?"

"Too late. They'll be well out over extra-territorial waters by now. There's no state of war. Not yet." He sighed. "Why, oh why, didn't I have an infrared movie camera tonight?"

Over in Mississippi Conde's task of breaking into the naval depot there turned out to be ridiculously easy. He had with him only six men, although he had sixteen more waiting in reserve aboard the 120-foot vessel *Roamer*, which was tied up dockside less than thirty feet from the arsenal. Those men had already effectively neutralized the three armed guards who patrolled the dock area at night.

The arsenal was guarded by only two retired naval petty officers, who regarded their job not only as a sinecure but downright nonsense, for who in his right mind would want to steal depth charges and naval guns? It was their invariable custom to prepare themselves for sleep immediately upon arrival, and asleep they soundly were when Conde and his men entered through the door they hadn't even bothered to lock.

They used two forklift trucks to trundle depth charges, light, dual-purpose antiaircraft guns, and a sufficiency of shells down to the dockside, then used one of the scores of cranes that lined the dockside to lower the stolen equipment into the hold of the *Roamer*, which was then battened down. Clearing customs was the merest formality. The customs official had seen the *Roamer* come and go so many times that they had long ago lost count. Besides, no one was going to have the temerity to inspect the oceangoing property of one of the very richest men in the world: the *Roamer* was Lord Worth's seismological survey vessel.

At its base not far from Havana, a small, conventionally powered and Russian-built submarine slipped its moorings and quietly put out to sea. The hastily assembled but nonetheless hand-picked crew was informed that they were on a training cruise designed to test the seagoing readiness of Castro's tiny fleet. Not a man aboard believed a word of this.

Meanwhile Cronkite had not been idle. Unlike the others, he had no need to break into any place to obtain explosives. He had merely to use his own key. As the world's top expert in capping blazing gushers he had access to an unlimited number and great variety of explosives. He made a selection of those and had them trucked down to Galveston from Houston, where he lived; apart from the fact that Houston was the oil-rig center of the South, the nature of Cronkite's business made it essential for him to live within easy reach of an airport with international connections.

As the truck was on its way, another seismo-

logical vessel, a converted coast guard cutter, was
also closing in on Galveston. Without explaining
his reasons for needing the vessel, Cronkite had
obtained it through the good offices of Durant,
who had represented the Galveston-area companies at the meeting of the ten at Lake Tahoe.
The cutter, which went by the name of *Tiburon*,
was normally based at Freeport, and Cronkite
could quite easily have taken the shipment there,
but this would not have suited his purpose. The
tanker *Crusader* was unloading at Galveston,
and the *Crusader* was one of the three tankers
that plied regularly between the *Seawitch* and
the Gulf ports.

The *Tiburon* and Cronkite arrived almost
simultaneously sometime after midnight. Mulhooney, the *Tiburon*'s skipper, eased his ship
into a berth conveniently close to the *Crusader*.
Mulhooney was not the regular captain of the
Tiburon. That gentleman had been so overcome
by the sight of two thousand dollars in cash that
he had fallen ill, and would remain so for a
few days. Cronkite had recommended his friend
Mulhooney. Cronkite didn't immediately go
aboard the *Tiburon*. Instead he chatted with a
night-duty dock inspector, who watched with an
idle eye as what were obviously explosives were
transferred to the *Tiburon*. The two men had
known each other for years. Apart from observ-
ing that someone out in the Gulf must have been
careless with matches again, the port official had

no further pertinent comment to make. In response to idle questioning, Cronkite learned that the *Crusader* had finished off-loading its cargo and would be sailing in approximately one hour.

He boarded the *Tiburon,* greeted Mulhooney and went straight to the crew's mess. Seated among the others at this early hour were three divers already fully clad in wetsuits. He gave brief instructions and the three men went on deck. Under cover of the superstructure and on the side of the ship remote from the dock the three men donned scuba gear, went down a rope ladder and slid quietly into the water. Six objects—radio-detonated magnetic mines equipped with metallic clamps—were lowered to them. They were so constructed as to have a very slight negative buoyancy, which made them easy to tow under water.

In the predawn darkness the hulls of the vessels cast so heavy a shadow from the powerful shorelights that the men could have swum unobserved on the surface. But Cronkite was not much given to taking chances. The mines were attached along the stern half of the *Crusader*'s hull, thirty feet apart and at a depth of about ten feet. Five minutes after their departure the scuba divers were back. After a further five minutes the *Tiburon* put out to sea.

Despite his near-legendary reputation for ruthlessness, Cronkite had not lost touch with humanity: to say that he was possessed of an innate kindliness would have been a distortion of the truth, for he was above all an uncompromising and single-minded realist, but one with no innate killer instinct. Nonetheless, there were two things that would at that moment have given him considerable satisfaction.

The first of those was that he would have preferred to have the *Crusader* at sea before pressing the sheathed button before him on the bridge. He had no wish that innocent lives should be lost in Galveston, but it was a chance that he had to take. Limpet mines, as the Italian divers had proved at Alexandria in World War II—and this to the great distress of the Royal Navy—could be devastatingly effective against moored vessels. But what might happen to high-buoyancy limpets when a ship got under way and worked up to maximum speed was impossible to forecast, as there was no known case of a vessel under way having been destroyed by limpet mines. It was at least possible that water pressure on a ship under way might well overcome the tenuous magnetic hold of the limpets and tear them free.

The second temptation was to board the helicopter on the *Tiburon*'s after helipad—many such vessels carried helicopters for the purpose of having them drop patterned explosives on the seabed to register on the seismological computer—and have a close look at what would be the ensuing havoc, a temptation he immediately regarded as pure self-indulgence.

He put both thoughts from his mind. Eight miles out from Galveston he unscrewed the covered switch and leaned firmly on the button beneath. The immediate results were wholly unspectacular, and Cronkite feared that they might be out of radio range. But in the port area in Galveston the results were highly spectacular. Six shattering explosions occurred almost simultaneously, and within twenty seconds the *Crusader,* her stern section torn in half, developed a marked list to starboard as thousands of tons of water poured through the ruptured side. Another twenty seconds later the distant rumble of the explosions reached the ears of listeners on the *Tiburon.* Cronkite and Mulhooney, alone on the bridge—the ship was on automatic pilot— looked at each other with grim satisfaction. Mulhooney, an Irishman with a true Irishman's sense of occasion, produced an opened bottle of champagne and poured two brimming glassfuls. Cronkite, who normally detested the stuff, consumed his drink with considerable relish and set his glass down. It was then that the *Crusader* caught fire.

Its gasoline tanks, true, were empty, but its engine diesel fuel tanks were almost completely topped up. In normal circumstances ignited diesel does not explode but burns with a ferocious intensity. Within seconds the smoke-veined flames had risen to a height of two hundred feet, the height increasing with each moment until the whole city was bathed in a crimson glow, a phenomenon which the citizens of Galveston had never seen before and would almost certainly never see again. Even aboard the *Tiburon* the spectacle had an awe-inspiring and unearthly quality about it. Then, as suddenly as it had begun, the fire stopped as the *Crusader* turned completely over on its side, the harbor waters quenching the flames into hissing extinction. Some patches of floating oil still flickered feebly across the harbor, but that was all that there was to it.

Clearly Lord Worth was going to require a new tanker, a requirement that presented quite a problem. In this area of a gross oversupply of tankers, any one of scores of laid-up super-tankers could be had just through exercising enough strength to lift a telephone. But 50,000-ton tankers, though not a dying breed, were a dwindling breed, principally because the main shipyards throughout the world had stopped producing them. "Had" is the operative word. Keels of that size and even smaller were now being hastily laid down, but would not be in full operation for a year or two to come. The reason was perfectly simple. Supertankers on the Arabian Gulf-Europe run had to make the long and prohibitively expensive circuit around the Cape of Good Hope because the newly reopened Suez Canal could not accommodate their immense draft, a problem that presented no difficulties to smaller tankers. It was said, and probably with more than a grain of truth, that the notoriously wily Greek shipowners had established a corner on this particular market.

The dawn was in the sky.

At that precise moment there were scenes of considerable activity around and aboard the *Seawitch*. The Panamanian-registered tanker *Torbello* was just finishing off-loading the contents of the *Seawitch*'s massive floating conical oil tank. As they were doing so, two helicopters appeared over the northeastern horizon. Both were very large Sikorsky machines which had been bought by the thrifty Lord Worth for the traditional song, not because they were obsolete but because they were two of the scores that had become redundant since the end of the Vietnam War, and the armed forces had been only too anxious to get rid of them: civilian demand for ex-gunships is not high.

The first of those to land on the helipad debarked twenty-two men, led by Lord Worth and Giuseppe Palermo. The other twenty, who from their appearance were not much given to caring for widows and orphans, all carried with them the impeccable credentials of oil experts of one type or another. That they were experts was beyond question; what was equally beyond question was that none of them would have recognized a barrel of oil if he had fallen into it. They were experts in diving, underwater demolition, the handling of high explosives, and the accurate firing of a variety of unpleasant weapons.

The second helicopter arrived immediately after the first had taken off. Except for the pilot and copilot, it carried no other human cargo. What it did carry was the immense and varied quantity of highly offensive weapons from the Florida arsenal, the loss of which had not yet been reported in the newspapers.

The oil-rig crew watched the arrival of gunmen and weapons with an oddly dispassionate curiosity. They were men to whom the unusual was familiar; the odd, the incongruous, the inexplicable, part and parcel of their daily lives. Oil-rig crews are a race apart, and Lord Worth's men formed a very special subdivision of that race.

Lord Worth called them all together, told of the threat to the *Seawitch* and the defensive measures he was undertaking, measures which were thoroughly approved of by the crew, who had as much regard for their own skins as had the rest of mankind. Lord Worth finished by saying that he knew he had no need to swear them to secrecy.

In this the noble Lord was perfectly correct. Though they were all experienced, hardly a man aboard had not at one time or another had a close and painful acquaintanceship with the law. There were ex-convicts among them. There were escaped convicts among them. There were those whom the law was very anxious to interview. And there were parolees who had broken their parole. There could be no safer hideouts for those men than the *Seawitch* and Lord Worth's privately owned motel where they put up during their off-duty spells. No law officer in his sane mind was going to question the towering respectability and integrity of one of the most powerful oil barons in the world, and by inevitable implication this attitude of mind extended to those in his employ.

In other words, Lord Worth, through the invaluable intermediacy of Commander Larsen, picked his men with extreme care.

Accommodation for the newly arrived men and storage for the weaponry presented no problem. Like many jack-ups, drill ships and submersibles, the *Seawitch* had two complete sets of accommodation and messes—one for Westerners, the other for Orientals: there were at that time no Orientals aboard.

Lord Worth, Commander Larsen and Palermo held their own private council of war in the luxuriously equipped sitting room which Lord Worth kept permanently reserved for himself. They agreed on everything. They agreed that Cronkite's campaign against them would be distinguished by a noticeable lack of subtlety: outright violence was the only course open to him. Once the oil was off-loaded ashore, there was nothing Cronkite could do about it. He would not attempt to attack and sink a loaded tanker, just as he would not attempt to destroy their huge floating storage tank. Either method would cause a massive oil slick, comparable to or probably exceeding the great oil slick caused by the Torrey Canyon disaster off the southwest coast of England some years previously. The ensuing international uproar would be bound to uncover something, and if Cronkite were implicated he would undoubtedly implicate the major oil companies—who wouldn't like that at all. And that there would be a massive investigation was inevitable: ecology and pollution were still the watchwords of the day.

Cronkite could attack the flexible oil pipe that connected the rig with the tank, but the three men agreed that this could be taken care of. After Conde and the *Roamer* arrived and its cargo had been hoisted aboard, the *Roamer* would maintain a constant day-and-night patrol between the rig and the tank. The *Seawitch* was well-equipped with sensory devices, apart from those which controlled the tensioning anchor cables. A radar scanner was in constant operation atop the derrick, and sonar devices were attached to each of the three giant legs some twenty feet under water. The radar could detect any hostile approach from air or sea, and the dual-purpose antiaircraft guns, aboard and installed, could take care of those. In the highly unlikely event of an underwater attack, sonar would locate the source, and a suitably placed depth charge from the *Roamer* would attend to that.

Lord Worth, of course, was unaware that at that very moment another craft was moving out at high speed to join Cronkite on the *Tiburon*. It was a standard and well-established design irreverently known as the "push-pull," in which water was ducted in through a tube forward under the hull and forced out under pressure at the rear. It had no propeller and had been designed primarily for work close inshore or in swamps, where there was always the danger of the propeller being fouled. The only difference between this vessel—the *Starlight*—and others was that it was equipped with a bank of storage batteries and could be electrically powered. Sonar could detect and accurately pinpoint a ship's engines and propeller vibrations; it was virtually helpless against an electric push-pull.

Lord Worth and the others considered the possibility of a direct attack on the *Seawitch*. Because of her high degree of compartmentalization and her great positive buoyancy, nothing short of an atom bomb was capable of disposing of something as large as a football field. Certainly no conventional weapon could. The attack, when it came, would be localized. The drilling derrick was an obvious target, but how Cronkite could approach it unseen could not be imagined. But Lord Worth was certain of one thing: when the attack came it would be leveled against the *Seawitch*.

The next half hour was to prove, twice, just how wrong Lord Worth could be.

The first intimations of disaster came as Lord Worth was watching the fully laden *Torbello* just disappearing over the northern horizon; the *Crusader,* he knew, was due alongside the tank late that afternoon. Larsen, his face one huge scowl of fury, silently handed Lord Worth a signal just received in the radio office. Lord Worth read it, and his subsequent language would have disbarred him forever from a seat in the House of Lords. The message told, in cruelly unsparing fashion, of the spectacular end of the *Crusader* in Galveston.

Both men hurried to the radio room. Larsen contacted the *Jupiter,* their third tanker then off-loading at an obscure Louisiana port, told its captain the unhappy fate of the *Crusader* and warned him to have every man on board on constant lookout until they had cleared harbor.

Lord Worth personally called the chief of police in Galveston, identified himself and demanded more details of the sinking of the *Crusader*. These he duly received, and none of them made him any happier. On inspiration, he asked if there had been a man called John Cronkite or a vessel belonging to a man of that name in the vicinity at the time. He was told to hang on while a check was made with Customs. Two minutes later he was told yes, there had been a John Cronkite aboard a vessel called the *Tiburon,* which had been moored directly aft of the *Crusader.* It was not known whether Cronkite was the owner or not. The *Tiburon* had sailed half an hour before the *Crusader* blew up.

Lord Worth peremptorily demanded that the *Tiburon* be apprehended and returned to port and that Cronkite be arrested. The police chief pointed out that international law prohibited the arrest of vessels on the high seas except in time of war and, as for Cronkite, there wasn't a shred of evidence to connect him with the sinking of the *Crusader.* Lord Worth then asked if he would trace the owner of the *Tiburon.* This the police chief promised to do, but warned that there might be a considerable delay. There were many registers to be consulted.

At that moment the Cuban submarine steaming on the surface at full speed was in the vicinity of Key West and heading directly for the *Seawitch.* At almost the same time a missile-armed Russian destroyer slipped its moorings in Havana and set off in apparent pursuit of the Cuban submarine. And very shortly after that, a destroyer departed its home base in Venezuela.

The *Roamer,* Lord Worth's survey vessel

under the command of Conde, was now halfway to its destination.

The *Starlight*, under the command of Easton, was just moving away from the *Tiburon*, which was lying stopped in the water. Men on slings had already painted out the ship's name, and with the aid of cardboard stencils were painting in a new name—*Georgia*. Cronkite had no wish that any vessel with whom they might make contact could radio for confirmation of the existence of a cutter called *Tiburon*. From aft there came the unmistakable racket of a helicopter engine starting up, then the machine took off, circled and headed southeast, not on its usual pattern-bombing circuit but to locate and radio back to the *Tiburon* the location and course of the *Torbello*, if and when it found it. Within minutes the *Tiburon* was on its way again, heading in approximately the same direction as the helicopter.

Chapter 4

*L*ORD Worth, enjoying a very early morning cup of tea, was in his living room with Larsen and Palermo when the radio operator knocked and entered, a message sheet in his hand. He handed it to Lord Worth and said: "For you, sir. But it's in some sort of code. Do you have a code book?"

"No need." Lord Worth smiled with some self-satisfaction, his first smile of any kind for quite some time. "I invented this code myself." He tapped his head. "Here's my code book."

The operator left. The other two watched in mild anticipation as Lord Worth began to decode. The anticipation turned into apprehension as the smile disappeared from Lord Worth's face, and the apprehension gave way in turn to deep concern as reddish-purple spots the size of pennies touched either cheekbone. He laid down the message sheet, took a deep breath, then proceeded to give a repeat performance—though this time more deeply felt, more impassioned—of the unparliamentary language he had used at the news of the loss of the *Crusader*. After some time he desisted, less because he had nothing fresh to say than from sheer loss of breath.

Larsen had more wit than to ask Lord Worth if something were the matter. Instead he said in a quiet voice: "Suppose you tell us, Lord Worth?"

Lord Worth, with no little effort, composed himself and said: "It seems that Cor—" He broke off and corrected himself: it was one of his many axioms that the right hand shouldn't know what the left hand doeth. "I was informed—all too reliably, as it now appears—that a couple of countries hostile to us might well be prepared to use naval force against us. One, it appears, is already prepared to do so. A destroyer has just cleared its Venezuelan home port and is heading in what is approximately our direction."

"They wouldn't dare," Palermo said.

"When people are power- and money-mad they'll stop at nothing." It apparently never occurred to Lord Worth that his description of people applied, *in excelsis,* to himself.

"Who's the other power?" said Larsen.

"The Soviet Union."

"Is it now?" Larsen seemed quite unmoved. "I don't know if I like the sound of that."

"We could do without them." Lord Worth was back on balance again. He flipped out a notebook and consulted it. "I think I'll have a talk with Washington." His hand was just reaching out for the phone when it rang. He lifted the instrument, at the same time turning the switch that cut the incoming call into the bulkhead speaker.

"Worth."

A vaguely disembodied voice came through the speaker. "You know who I am?" Disembodied or not, the voice was known to Worth. Corral.

"Yes."

"I've checked my contact, sir. I'm afraid our guesses were only too accurate. Both X and Y are willing to commit themselves to naval support."

"I know. One of them has just moved out and appears to be heading in our general direction."

"Which one?"

"The one to the south. Any talk of air commitment?"

"None that I've heard, sir. But I don't have to tell you that that doesn't rule out its use."

"Let me know if there is any more good news."

"Naturally. Goodbye, sir."

Lord Worth replaced the instrument, then lifted it again.

"I want a number in Washington."

"Can you hold a moment, sir?"

"Why?"

"There's another code message coming through. Looks like the same code as the last one, sir."

"I shouldn't be surprised." Lord Worth's tone was somber. "Bring it across as soon as possible."

He replaced the phone, pressed a button on the small console before him, lifting the phone again as he did.

"Chambers?" Chambers was his senior pilot.

"Sir?"

"Your chopper refueled?"

"Ready to go when you are, sir."

"May be any second now. Stand by your phone." He replaced the receiver.

Larsen said: "Washington beckons, sir?"

"I have the odd feeling that it's about to. There are things that one can achieve in person that one can't over the phone. Depends upon this next message."

"If you go, anything to be done in your absence?"

"There'll be dual-purpose antiaircraft guns arriving aboard the *Roamer* this afternoon. Secure them to the platform."

"To the north, south, east but not west?"

"As you wish."

"We don't want to start blowing holes in our own oil tank."

"There's that. There'll also be mines. Three piles, each halfway between a pair of legs."

"An underwater explosion from a mine wouldn't damage the legs?"

"I shouldn't think so. We'll just have to find out, won't we? Keep in constant half-hourly touch with both the *Torbello* and the *Jupiter*. Keep the radar and sonar stations constantly manned. Eternal vigilance, if you will. Hell, Commander, I don't have to tell you what to do." He wrote some figures on a piece of paper. "If I do have to go, contact this number in Washington. Tell them that I'm coming. Five hours or so."

"This is the State Department?"

"Yes. Tell them that at least the Under Secretary must be there. Remind him, tactfully, of future campaign contributions. Then contact my aircraft pilot, Dawson. Tell him to be standing by with a filed flight plan for Washington."

The radio operator knocked, entered, handed Lord Worth a message sheet and left. Lord Worth, hands steady and face now untroubled, decoded the message, reached for the phone and told Chambers to get to the helicopter at once.

He said to the two men: "A Russian-built Cuban submarine is on its way from Havana. It's being followed by a Russian guided-missile destroyer. Both are heading this way."

"A visit to the State Department or the Pentagon would appear to be indicated," Larsen said. "There isn't too much we can do about guided missiles. Looks like there might be quite some activity hereabouts. That makes five vessels arrowing in on us—three naval vessels, the *Jupiter* and the *Roamer*." Larsen might have been even more concerned had he known that the number of vessels was seven, not five: but, then, Larsen was not to know that the *Tiburon* and the *Starlight* were heading that way also.

Lord Worth rose. "Well, keep an eye on the shop. Back this evening sometime. I'll be in frequent radio contact."

Lord Worth was to fly four legs that day: by helicopter to the mainland, by his private Boeing to Washington, the return flight to Florida, and the final leg by helicopter out to the *Seawitch*. On each of those four legs something very unpleasant was going to happen—unpleasant for Lord Worth, that is. Fortunately for Lord Worth, he was not blessed with the alleged Scottish second sight—the ability to look into the future.

The first of those unpleasantnesses happened when Lord Worth was en route to the mainland. A large station wagon swept up to the front door of Lord Worth's mansion, carrying five rather large men who would have been difficult later to identify, for all five wore stocking masks. One of them carried what appeared to be a large coil of clothesline rope, another a roll of adhesive tape. All carried guns.

MacPherson, the elderly head gardener, was taking his customary prework dawn patrol to see what damage the fauna had wreaked on his flora during the night, when the men emerged from the station wagon. Even allowing for the fact that shock had temporarily paralyzed his vocal cords, he never had a chance. In just over a minute, bound hand and foot and with his lips sealed with adhesive tape, he had been dumped unceremoniously into a clump of bushes.

The leader of the group, a man by the name of Durand, pressed the front-door bell. Durand, a man who had a powerful affinity with banks and who was a three-time ex-convict, was by definition a man of dubious reputation, a reputation confirmed by the fact that he was a close and longtime term associate of Cronkite. Half a minute passed, then he rang again. By and by the door opened to reveal a robe-wrapped Jenkins, tousle-haired and blinking the sleep from his eyes—it was still very early in the morning. His eyes stopped blinking and opened wide when he saw the pistol in Durand's hand.

Durand touched the cylinder screwed onto the muzzle of his gun. As hooked a TV addict as the next man, Jenkins recognized a silencer when he saw one.

"You know what this is?"

A fully awake Jenkins nodded silently.

"We don't want to harm anyone in the house. Especially, no harm will come to you if you do what you are told. Doing what you are told includes not telling lies. Understood?"

Jenkins understood.

"How many staff do you have here?"

There was a noticeable quaver in Jenkins's voice. "Well, there's me—I'm the butler—"

Durand was patient. "You we can see."

"Two footmen, a chauffeur, a radio operator, a secretary, a cook and two housemaids. There's a cleaning lady, but she doesn't come until eight."

"Tape him," Durand said. Jenkins's lips were taped. "Sorry about that, but people can be silly at times. Take us to those eight bedrooms."

Jenkins reluctantly led the way. Ten minutes later, all eight of the staff were securely bound and silenced. Durand said: "And now, the two young ladies."

Jenkins led them to a door. Durand picked out three of his men and said softly: "The butler will take you to the other girl. Check what she packs and especially her purse."

Durand, followed by his men, entered the room, his gun in its concealed holster so as not to arouse too much alarm. That the bed was occupied was beyond doubt, although all that could be seen was a mop of black hair on the pillow. Durand said in a conversational voice: "I think you better get up, ma'am." Durand was not normally given to gentleness, but he did not want a case of screaming hysterics on his hands.

A case of hysterics he did not have. Marina turned round in bed and looked at him with drowsy eyes. The drowsiness did not last long. The eyes opened wide, either in fear or shock, then returned to normal. She reached for a robe, arranged it strategically on the bed cover, then sat bolt upright, wrapping the robe round her.

"Who are you and what do you want?" Her voice was not quite as steady as she might have wished.

"Well, would you look at that, now?" Durand said admiringly. "You'd think she was used to being kidnaped every morning of her life."

"This is a kidnap?"

"I'm afraid so." Durand sounded genuinely apologetic.

"Where are you taking me?"

"Vacation. Little island in the sun." Durand smiled. "You won't be needing any swimsuit though. Please get up and get dressed."

"And if I refuse?"

"We'll dress you."

"I'm not going to get dressed with you two watching me."

Durand was soothing. "My friend will stand out in the corridor. I'll go into the bathroom there and leave the door open just a crack—not to watch you, but to watch the window, to make sure that you don't leave by it. Call me when you're ready and be quick about it."

She was quick about it. She called him within three minutes. Blue blouse, blue slacks and her hair combed. Durand nodded his approval.

"Pack a traveling bag. Enough for a few days."

He watched her while she packed. She zipped the bag shut and picked up her purse. "I'm ready."

He took the purse from her, undid the clasp and upended the contents on the bed. From the jumble on the bed he selected a small pearl-handled pistol, which he slipped into his pocket.

"Let's pack the purse again, shall we?"

Marina did so, her face flushed with mortification.

A somewhat similar scene had just taken place in Melinda's bedroom.

Twenty-five minutes had elapsed since the arrival of Durand and his men and their departure with the two girls. No one had been hurt, except in pride, and the intruders had even been considerate to the extent of seating Jenkins in a deep armchair in the front hall. Jenkins, as he was now securely bound hand and foot, did not appreciate this courtesy as much as he might have done.

About ten minutes after their departure, Lord Worth's helicopter touched down beside his

Boeing in the city airport. There were no customs, no clearance formalities. Lord Worth had made it plain some years previously that he did not much care for that sort of thing, and when Lord Worth made things plain they tended to remain that way.

It was during the second leg of this flight that the second unfortunate occurrence happened. Again, Lord Worth was happily unaware of what was taking place.

The *Tiburon*'s (now the *Georgia*'s) helicopter had located the *Torbello*. The pilot reported that he had sighted the vessel two minutes previously and gave her latitude and longitude as accurately as he could judge. More importantly, he gave her course as approximately 315 degrees, which was virtually on a collision course with the *Georgia*. They were approximately forty-five miles apart. Cronkite gave his congratulations to the pilot and asked him to return to the *Georgia*.

On the bridge of the *Georgia* Cronkite and Mulhooney looked at each other with satisfaction. Between planning and execution there often exists an unbridgeable gap. In this case, however, things appeared to be going exactly according to plan.

Cronkite said to Mulhooney: "Time, I think, to change into more respectable clothes. And don't forget to powder your nose."

Mulhooney smiled and left the bridge. Cronkite paused only to give a few instructions to the helmsman, then left the bridge also.

Less than an hour later the *Torbello* stood clear over the horizon. The *Georgia* headed straight for it, then at about three miles distance made a thirty-degree alteration to starboard, judged the timing to a nicety and came round in a wide sweeping turn to port. Two minutes later the *Georgia* was on a parallel course to the *Torbello*, alongside its port quarter—the bridge of a tanker lies very far aft—paralleling its course at the same speed and not more than thirty yards away. Cronkite moved out onto the wing of the *Georgia*'s bridge and lifted his loud-hailer.

"Coast Guard. Please stop. This is a request, not an order. We think your vessel's in great danger. Your permission, please, to bring a trained research party aboard. For the safety of your men and the ship, don't break radio silence on any account!"

Captain Thompson, an honest sailor with no criminal propensities whatsoever, used his own loud-hailer.

"What's wrong? Why is this boarding necessary?"

"It's not a boarding. I am making a request for your own good. Believe me, I'd rather not be within five miles of you. It *is* necessary. I'd rather come aboard with my lieutenant and explain privately. Don't forget what happened to your sister ship, the *Crusader,* in Galveston harbor last night."

Captain Thompson, clearly, had not forgotten and was, of course, completely unaware that Cronkite was the man responsible for what had happened to his sister ship: a ringing of bells from the bridge was indication enough of that. Three minutes later the *Torbello* lay stopped in the calm waters. The *Georgia* edged up alongside the *Torbello* until its midships were just ahead of the bulk of the tanker's superstructure. At this point it was possible to step from the *Georgia's* deck straight onto the deck of the deep-laden tanker, which was what Cronkite and Mulhooney proceeded to do. They paused there until they had made sure that the *Georgia* was securely moored fore and aft to the tanker, then climbed a series of companionways and ladders up to the bridge.

Both men were quite unrecognizable. Cronkite had acquired a splendidly bushy black beard, a neatly trimmed mustache and dark glasses and, with his smartly tailored uniform and slightly rakish peaked cap, looked the epitome of the competent and dashing coast-guard-cutter captain which he was not. Mulhooney was similarly disguised.

There was only Captain Thompson and an idle

helmsman on the bridge. Cronkite shook the captain's hand.

"Good morning. Sorry to disturb you when you are proceeding about your lawful business and all that, but you may be glad we stopped you. First, where is your radio room?" Captain Thompson nodded to a door set in back of the bridge. "I'd like my lieutenant to check on the radio silence. This is imperative." Again, Captain Thompson, now feeling distinctly uneasy, nodded. Cronkite looked at Mulhooney. "Go check, Dixon, will you?"

Mulhooney passed through into the radio room, closing the door behind him. The radio operator looked up from his transceiver with an air of mild surprise.

"Sorry to disturb." Mulhooney sounded almost genial, a remarkable feat for a man totally devoid of geniality. "I'm from the Coast Guard cutter alongside. The captain told you to keep radio silence?"

"That's just what I'm doing."

"Made any radio calls since leaving the *Seawitch?*"

"Only the routine half-hourly on-course, on-time calls."

"Do they acknowledge those? I have my reasons for asking." Mulhooney carefully refrained from saying what his reasons were.

"No. Well, just the usual 'roger and out' business."

"What's the call-up frequency?"

The operator pointed to the console. "Preset."

Mulhooney nodded and walked casually behind the operator. Just to make sure that the operator kept on maintaining radio silence, Mulhooney clipped him over the right ear with his pistol. He then returned to the bridge, where he found Captain Thompson in a state of considerable and understandable perturbation.

Captain Thompson, a deep anxiety compounded by a self-defensive disbelief, said: "What you're telling me in effect is that the *Torbello* is a floating time bomb."

"A bomb, certainly. Maybe lots of bombs. Not only possible but almost certain. Our sources of information—sorry, I'm not at liberty to divulge those—are as nearly perfect as can be."

"God's sake, man, no one would be so crazy as to cause a huge oil slick in the Gulf."

Cronkite said: "It's your assumption, not mine, that we're dealing with sane minds. Who but a crazy man would have endangered Galveston by blowing up your sister tanker there?"

The captain fell silent and pondered the question gloomily.

Cronkite went on: "Anyway, it's my intention—with your consent, of course—to search the engine room, living accommodations and every storage space on the ship. With the kind of search crew I have it shouldn't take more than half an hour."

"What kind of preset time bomb do you think it might be?"

"I don't think it's a time bomb—or bombs—at all. I think that the detonator—or detonators—will be a certain radioactivated device that can be triggered by any nearby craft, plane or helicopter. But I don't think it's fixing to happen till you're close to the U.S. coast."

"Why?"

"So we'll have maximum pollution along the shores. There'll be a national holler against Lord Worth and the safety standards aboard his—ah—rather superannuated tankers, maybe resulting in closing down the *Seawitch* or the seizing of any of Worth's tankers that might enter American territorial waters." In addition to his many other specialized qualifications, Cronkite was a consummate liar. "Okay if I call my men?" Captain Thompson nodded without any noticeable enthusiasm.

Cronkite lifted the loud-hailer and ordered the search party aboard. They came immediately, fourteen of them, all of them wearing stocking masks, all of them carrying machine pistols. Captain Thompson stared at them in stupefaction; then turned and stared some more at Cronkite and Mulhooney, both of whom had pistols leveled at him. Cronkite may have been looking satisfied or even triumphant, but such was the abundance of his ersatz facial foliage that it was impossible to tell.

Captain Thompson, in a stupefaction that was slowly turning into a slow burn, said: "What the hell goes?"

"You can see what goes. Hijack. A very popular pastime nowadays. I agree that nobody's ever hijacked a tanker before, but there always has to be a first time. Besides, it's not really something new. Piracy on the high seas. They've been at it for thousands of years. Don't try anything rash, Captain, and please don't try to be a hero. If you all behave, no harm will come to you. Anyway, what could you possibly do with fourteen submachine guns lined up against you?"

Within five minutes all the crew, officers and men, including the recovered radio operator but with one other exception, were herded into the crew's mess under armed guard. Nobody had even as much as contemplated offering resistance. The exception was an unhappy-looking duty engineer in the engine room. There are few people who don't look slightly unhappy when staring at the muzzle of a Schmeisser from a distance of five feet.

Cronkite was on the bridge giving Mulhooney his final instructions.

"Keep on sending the *Seawitch* its half-hour on-time, on-course reports. Then report a minor breakdown in two or three hours—a fractured fuel line or something of the sort—enough that would keep the *Torbello* immobilized for a few hours. You're due in Galveston tonight and I need time and room to maneuver. Rather, *you* need time and room to maneuver. When it gets dark keep every navigational light extinguished —in fact, *every* light extinguished. Let's don't underestimate Lord Worth." Cronkite was speaking with an unaccustomed degree of bitterness, doubtless recalling the day Lord Worth had taken him to the cleaners in court. "He's a very powerful man, and it's quite in the cards that he can have an air-and-sea search mounted for his missing tanker."

Cronkite rejoined the *Georgia,* cast off and pulled away. Mulhooney, too, got under way, but altered course ninety degrees to port so that he was heading southwest instead of northwest. On the first half hour he sent the reassuring report to the *Seawitch*—"on course, on time."

Cronkite waited for the *Starlight* to join him, then both vessels proceeded together in a generally southeasterly direction until they were about thirty-five nautical miles from the *Seawitch,* safely over the horizon and out of reach of the *Seawitch*'s radar and sonar. They stopped their engines and settled down to wait.

The big Boeing had almost halved the distance between Florida and Washington. Lord Worth, in his luxurious stateroom immediately abaft the flight deck, was making up for time lost during the previous night and, blissfully unaware of the slings and arrows that were coming at him from all sides, was soundly asleep.

Mitchell had been unusually but perhaps not unexpectedly late in waking that morning. He showered, shaved and dressed while the coffee percolated, all the time conscious of a peculiar and unaccustomed sense of unease. He paced up and down the kitchen, drinking his coffee, then abruptly decided to put his unease at rest. He lifted the phone and dialed Lord Worth's mansion. The other end rang, rang again and kept on ringing. Mitchell replaced the receiver, then tried again with the same result. He finished his coffee, went across to Roomer's house and let himself in with his passkey. He went into the bedroom to find Roomer still asleep. He woke him up. Roomer regarded him with disfavor.

"What do you mean by waking up a man in the middle of the night?"

"It's not the middle of the night." He pulled open the drapes and the bright summer sunlight flooded the room. "It's broad daylight, as you will be able to see when you open your eyes."

"Your house on fire or something, then?"

"I wish it were something as trivial as that. I'm worried, John. I woke up feeling bugged by something, and the feeling got worse and worse. Five minutes ago I called up Lord Worth's house. I tried twice. There was no reply. Must have been at least eight or ten people in that house, but there was no reply."

"What do you think—"

"You're supposed to be the man with the intuition. Get ready. I'll go make some coffee."

Long before the coffee was ready, in fact less than ninety seconds later, Roomer was in the kitchen. He had of course neither showered nor shaved but had had time to run a comb through his hair. He was looking the same way the expressionless Mitchell was feeling.

"Never mind the coffee." Roomer bore an almost savage expression on his face, but Mitchell knew that it wasn't directed at him. "Let's get up to the house."

They took Roomer's car; it was nearer.

Mitchell said: "God, we're really bright! Hit us over the head often enough and maybe—just maybe—we'll begin to see the obvious." He held on to his seat as Roomer, tires screeching, rounded a blind corner. "Easy, boy, easy. Too late to lock the stable now."

With what was a clearly conscious effort of will, Roomer slowed down. He said: "Yeah, we're real clever. Lord Worth used a threat of the girls' abduction as an excuse for his actions. And you told him to offer the threat of the abduction as an excuse for our being there last night. And it never occurred to either of our staggering intellects that their kidnaping would be both logical and inevitable. Worth wasn't

exaggerating—he has enemies, and vicious enemies who are out to get him. Two trump cards—
and what trumps! He's powerless now. He'll give
away half his money to get them back. Just half.
He'll use the other half to hunt those people
down. Money can buy any co-operation in the
world, and the old boy *has* all the money in the
world."

Mitchell now seemed relaxed, comfortable,
even calm. He said: "But we'll get to them first,
won't we, John?"

Roomer stirred uncomfortably in his seat as
they swung into the mansion's driveway. He said:
"I'm just as sore as you are. But I don't like it
when you start talking that way. You know
that."

"I'm expressing an intention—or at least a
hope." He smiled. "We'll see."

Roomer stopped his car in a fashion that did
little good to Lord Worth's immaculately raked
gravel. The first thing that caught Mitchell's eye
as he left the car was an odd movement by the
side of the driveway in a clump of bushes. He
took out his gun and went to investigate, then put
his gun away, opened his clasp knife and sliced
through MacPherson's bonds. The head gardener, after forty years in Florida, had never lost
a trace of a very pronounced Scottish accent, an
accent that tended to thicken according to the
degree of mental stress he was undergoing. On
this occasion, with the adhesive removed, his

language was wholly indecipherable—which, in view of what he was almost certainly trying to say, was probably just as well.

They went through the front doorway. Jenkins, apparently taking his ease in a comfortable armchair, greeted them with a baleful glare. The glare was in no way intended for them; Jenkins was just in a baleful mood, a mood scarcely bettered by Mitchell's swift and painful yanking away of the adhesive from his lips. Jenkins took a deep breath, preparatory to lodging some form of protest, but Mitchell cut in before he could speak.

"Where does Jim sleep?" Jim was the radio operator.

Jenkins stared at him in astonishment. Was this the way to greet a man who had been through a living hell—snatched, one might almost say, from the jaws of death? Where was the sympathy, the condolence, the anxious questioning? Mitchell put his hands on his shoulders and shook him violently.

"Are you deaf? Jim's room?"

Jenkins looked at the grim face less than a foot from his own and decided against remonstrating. "In back, first floor, first right."

Mitchell left. So, after a second or two, did Roomer. Jenkins called after him in a plaintive voice: "You aren't leaving me too, Mr. Roomer?"

Roomer turned and said patiently: "I'm going to the kitchen to get a nice sharp carver. Mr.

Mitchell has taken the only knife we have between us."

Jim Robertson was young, fresh-faced and just out of college, a graduate in electrical engineering in no hurry to proceed with his profession. He sat on the bed massaging his now unbound wrists, wincing slightly as the circulation began to return. As tiers of knots, Durand's henchmen had been nothing if not enthusiastic.

Mitchell said: "How do you feel?"

"Mad."

"I don't blame you. Are you okay to operate your set?"

"I'm okay for anything if it means getting hold of those bastards."

"That's the general idea. Did you get a good look at the kidnapers?"

"I can give you a general description." He broke off and stared at Mitchell. *"Kidnapers?"*

"Looks as though Lord Worth's daughters have been abducted."

"Holy Christ!" The assimilation of this news took some little time. "There'll be all hell to pay for this."

"It should cause a considerable flap. Do you know where Marina's room is?"

"I'll show you."

Her room showed all signs of a hasty and unpremeditated departure. Cupboard doors were open, drawers the same, and some spilled clothing lay on the floor. Mitchell was interested in none of this. He quickly riffled through drawers in the room until he found what he had hoped to find—her States passport. He opened it and it was valid. He made a mental note that she had lied about her age—she was two years older than she claimed to be—returned the passport and hurried down to the radio room with Robertson, who unlocked the door to let them in. Robertson looked questioningly at Mitchell.

"The county police chief. His name is McGarrity. I don't want anyone else. Tell him you're speaking for Lord Worth. That should work wonders. Then let me take over."

Roomer entered while Robertson was trying to make contact. "Seven more of the staff, all suitably immobilized. Makes nine in all. I've left Jenkins to cut them loose. His hands are shaking so bad he'll probably slice an artery or two, but for me freeing elderly cooks and young housemaids is above and beyond the call of duty."

"They must have been carrying a mile of rope," Mitchell said absently. He was figuring out how much not to tell the police chief.

Roomer nodded to the operator. "Who's he trying to contact?"

"McGarrity."

"That hypocritical old brown-noser!"

"Most people would regard that as a charitable description. But he has his uses."

Robertson looked up. "On the line, Mr. Mitchell. That phone." He made discreetly to replace his own, but Roomer took it from him and listened in.

"Chief McGarrity?"

"Speaking."

"Please listen very carefully. This is extremely important and urgent, and the biggest thing that's ever come your way. Are you alone?"

"Yes. I'm all alone." McGarrity's tone held an odd mixture of suspicion and aroused interest.

"Nobody listening in, no recorder?"

"Goddam it, no. Get to the point."

"We're speaking from Lord Worth's house. You know of him?"

"Don't be a damned fool. Who's 'we'?"

"My name is Michael Mitchell. My partner is John Roomer. We're licensed private investigators."

"I've heard of you. You're the guys who give the local law so much trouble."

"I'd put it the other way around, but that's beside the point. What is to the point is that Lord Worth's two daughters have been kidnaped."

"Merciful God in heaven!" There ensued what could fairly have been described as a stunned silence at the other end of the line.

Roomer smiled sardonically and covered the mouthpiece. "Can't you see the old phony grabbing his seat, with his eyes popping and big signs saying 'Promotion' flashing in front of him?"

"Kidnaped, you said?" McGarrity's voice had suddenly developed a certain hoarseness.

"Kidnaped. Abducted. Snatched."

"Sure of this?"

"Sure as can be. The girls' rooms have all the signs of hurried and unplanned departure. Nine of the staff were bound and gagged. What would *you* conclude from that?"

"Kidnap." McGarrity made it sound as if he'd made the discovery all by himself.

"Can you put a block on all escape routes? They haven't taken the girls' passports, so that rules out international flights. I hardly think the kidnapers would have taken any commercial domestic flight. Can you see Lord Worth's daughters going through any airline terminal without being recognized? I'd put a stop order and guard at every private airfield and helicopter pad in the southern part of the state. And likewise at every port, big and small, in the same area."

McGarrity sounded bemused, befuddled. "That'd call for hundreds of policemen."

The tone of anguished protest was unmistakable. Mitchell sighed, cupped the mouthpiece, looked at Roomer and said: "Man's out of his depth. Can I call him lunkhead?" He removed his hand. "Look, Chief McGarrity, I don't think you realize what you're sitting on. We're talking about the daughters of Lord Worth. You could pick up your phone and get a thousand cops for

the asking. You could call out the National
Guard if you wanted to—I'm sure Lord Worth
would pick up the tab for every cent of expenses.
Good God, man, there's been nothing like this
since the Lindbergh kidnaping!"

"That's so, that's so." It wasn't difficult to vis-
ualize McGarrity licking his lips. "Descriptions?"

"Not much help there, I'm afraid. They all
wore stocking masks. The leader wore gloves,
which may or may not indicate a criminal record. All were big, well-built men and all wore
dark business suits. I don't have to give you a
description of the girls, I guess."

"Marina and Melinda?" McGarrity was a
classic snob of awesome proportions, who followed with avid interest the comings and goings
of alleged society, of the internationally famous
and infamous. "Hell, no. Of course not. They're
probably the most photographed pair in the
state."

"You'll keep this under wraps, tight as possible, for the moment?"

"I will, I will." McGarrity had his baby
clutched close to his heart, and nobody, but nobody was going to take it away from him.

"Lord Worth will have to be informed first of
all. I'll refer him to you."

"You mean you haven't told him yet?" Mc-
Garrity could hardly believe his good fortune.

"No."

"Tell him to take it easy—well, as easy as he

can, that is. Tell him I'm taking complete and personal charge of the investigation."

"I'll do that, Chief."

Roomer winced and screwed his eyes shut.

McGarrity sounded positively brisk. "Now, about the local law."

"I suppose I've got to call them in. I'm not too happy about it: they don't exactly like us. What if they refuse to keep this under wraps . . . ?"

"In which case," McGarrity said ominously, "just put the person concerned directly on the line to me. Anyone else know about this yet?"

"Of course not. You're the only man with the power to authorize the closing of the escape routes. Naturally we contacted you first."

"And you were perfectly right, Mr. Mitchell." McGarrity was warm and appreciative, as well he might have been, for he had a very shaky re-election coming up and the massive publicity the kidnaping was bound to generate would guarantee him a virtual shoo-in. "I'll get the wheels turning at this end. Keep me posted."

"Of course, Chief." Mitchell hung up.

Roomer looked at him admiringly. "You are an even bigger and stickier hypocrite than McGarrity."

"Practice. Anyway, we got what we wanted." Mitchell's face was somber. "Has it occurred to you that the birds may have flown?"

Roomer looked equally unhappy. "Yeah. But first things first. Lord Worth next?" Mitchell nodded. "I'll pass this one up. They say that, under provocation, he has a rich command of the English language, not at all aristocratic. I'd be better employed interviewing the staff. I'll ply them with strong drink to help them overcome the rigors of their ordeal and to loosen their tongues—Lord Worth's reserve Dom Perignon for choice—and see what I can get out of them. I don't expect much. All I can do is ask them about descriptions and voices and whether or not they touched anything that might give us fingerprints. Not that that will help if their prints aren't on file."

"The brandy bit sounds the best part of your program. Ask Jenkins to bring a large one"— he looked at Robertson—"*two* large ones."

Roomer was at the door when he turned. "Do you know what happened in ancient times to the bearers of bad news?"

"I know. They got their heads cut off."

"He'll probably blame us for carelessness and lack of foresight—and he'll be right, too, even though he's just as guilty as we are." Roomer left.

"Get me Lord Worth, Jim."

"I would if I knew where he was. He was here last night when I left."

"He's on the *Seawitch*."

Robertson raised an eyebrow, lowered it, said nothing and turned his attention to the switchboard. He raised the *Seawitch* in fifteen seconds. Mitchell took the phone.

"Lord Worth, please."

"Hold on."

Another voice came on, a rasping gravelly voice, not as friendly.

"What d'you want?"

"Lord Worth, please."

"How do you know he's here?"

"How do I—what does that matter? May I speak to him?"

"Look, mister, I'm here to protect Lord Worth's privacy. We get far too many oddball calls from oddball characters. How did you know he was here?"

"Because he told me."

"When?"

"Last night. About midnight."

"What's your name?"

"Mitchell. Michael Mitchell."

"Mitchell." Larsen's tone changed. "Why didn't you say so in the first place?"

"Because I didn't expect a Gestapo third degree, that's why. You must be Commander Larsen."

"That's me."

"Not very civil, are you?"

"I've got a job to do."

"Lord Worth."

"He's not here."

"He wouldn't lie to me." Mitchell thought it impolitic to add that he'd actually seen Lord Worth take off.

"He didn't lie to you. He was here. He left hours ago for Washington."

Mitchell was silent for a few moments while he considered. "Any number where he can be reached?"

"Yes. Why?"

"I didn't ask you why he'd gone to Washington. It's an urgent, private and personal matter. From what I've heard of you from Lord Worth, and that's quite a bit, you'd react in exactly the same way. Give me the number and I'll call back and fill you in just as soon as Lord Worth gives me clearance."

"Your word on that?"

Mitchell gave his promise and Larsen gave him the number.

Mitchell replaced the receiver. He said to Robertson: "Lord Worth has left the *Seawitch* and gone to Washington."

"He does get around. In his Boeing, I presume?"

"I didn't ask. I took that for granted. Do you think you can reach him on the plane?"

Robertson didn't look encouraging. "When did he leave the *Seawitch*?"

"I don't know. Should have asked, I suppose. Hours ago, Larsen said."

Robertson looked even more discouraged. "I wouldn't hold out any hope, Mr. Mitchell. With this set I can reach out a couple of thousand miles. Lord Worth's Boeing can reach any airport not quite as far away, just as the airport can reach him. But the receiving equipment aboard the Boeing hasn't been modified to receive long-range transmissions from this set, which is very specialized. Short-range only. Five hundred miles, if that. The Boeing is bound to be well out of range by now."

"Freak weather conditions?"

"Mighty rare, Mr. Mitchell."

"Try anyway, Jim."

He tried and kept on trying for five minutes, during which it became steadily more apparent that Lord Worth would have at least a bit more time before being set up for his coronary. At the end of five minutes Robertson shrugged his shoulders and looked up at Mitchell.

"Thanks for the try, Jim." He gave Robertson a piece of paper with a number on it. "Washington. Think you can reach that?"

"That I can guarantee."

"Try for it in half an hour. Ask for Lord Worth. Emphasize the urgency. If you don't contact him, try again every twenty minutes. You have a direct line to the study?"

"Yes."

"I'll be there. I have to welcome the law."

Lord Worth, still happily unaware of his disintegrating world, slept soundly. The Boeing, at thirty-three thousand feet, was just beginning its descent to Dulles Airport.

Chapter 5

*L*ORD Worth, a glass of scotch in one hand and an illegal Cuban cigar in the other, was comfortably ensconced in a deep armchair in the very plush office of the Assistant Secretary of State. He should have been contented and relaxed: he was, in fact, highly discontented and completely unrelaxed. He was becoming mad, steadily and far from slowly, at the world in general and at the four other people in that room in particular.

The four consisted of Howell, the Assistant Secretary, a tall, thin, keen-faced man with steel-framed glasses who looked like, and in fact was, a Yale professor. The second was his personal assistant, whose name, fittingly enough, Lord Worth had failed to catch, for he had about him the gray anonymity of a top-flight civil servant. The third was Lieutenant-General Zweicker, and all that could be said about him was that he looked every inch a general. The fourth was a middle-aged stenographer who appeared to take notes of the discussion whenever the mood struck her, which didn't appear to be very often: most likely, long experience had taught her that most of what was said at any conference wasn't worth noting anyway.

Lord Worth said: "I'm a very tired man who has just flown up from the Gulf of Mexico. I have spent twenty-five minutes here and appear to have wasted my time. Well, gentlemen, I have no intention of wasting my time. My time is as important as yours. Correction. It's a damn sight more important. 'The big brush-off,' I believe it's called."

"How can you call it a brush-off? You're sitting in my office and General Zweicker is here. How many other citizens rate that kind of treatment?"

"The bigger the façade, the bigger the brush-off. I am not accustomed to dealing with underlings. I am accustomed to dealing with the very top, which I haven't quite reached yet, but will. The cool, diplomatic, deep-freeze treatment will not work. I am no troublemaker, but I'll go any lengths to secure justice. You can't sweep me under your diplomatic carpet, Mr. Howell. I told you recently that there were international threats against the *Seawitch,* and you chose either to disbelieve me or ignore me. I come to you now with additional proof that I am threatened—three naval vessels heading for the *Seawitch*—and still you propose to take no action. And I would point out, incidentally, if you still don't know independently of the movements of those vessels, then it's time you got yourselves a new intelligence service."

General Zweicker said: "We are aware of those movements. But as yet we see no justification for taking any kind of action. You have no proof that what you claim is true. Suspicions, no more. Do you seriously expect us to alert naval units and a squadron of fighter-bombers on the unproven and what may well be the unfounded suspicions of a private citizen?"

"That's it in a nutshell," Howell said. "And I would remind you, Lord Worth, that you're not even an American citizen."

" 'Not even an American citizen.' " He turned to the stenographer. "I trust you made a note of that." He lifted his hand as Howell made to speak. "Too late, Howell. Too late to retrieve your blunder—a blunder, I may say, of classical proportions. Not an American citizen? I would point out that I paid more taxes last year than all your precious oil companies in the States combined—this apart from supplying the cheapest oil to the United States. If the level of competence of the State Department is typical of the way this country is run, then I can only rejoice in the fact that I still retain a British passport. One law for Americans, another for the heathen beyond the pale. Even-handed justice. 'Not an American citizen.' This should make a particularly juicy tidbit for the news conference I intend to hold immediately after I leave."

"A news conference?" Howell betrayed unmistakable signs of agitation.

"Certainly." Lord Worth's tone was as grim as his face. "If you people won't protect me, then, by God, I'll protect myself."

Howell looked at the general, then back to Lord Worth. He strove to inject an official and intimidating note into his voice. "I would remind you that any discussions that take place here are strictly confidential."

Lord Worth eyed him coldly. "It's always sad to see a man who has missed his true vocation. You should have been a comedian, Howell, not a senior member of government. Confidential. That's good. How can you remind me of something you never even mentioned before? Confidential. If there wasn't a lady present I'd tell you what I really think of your asinine remark. God, it's rich, a statement like that coming from the number two in a government department with so splendid a record of leaking state secrets to muckraking journalists, doubless in return for a suitable *quid pro quo*. I cannot abide hypocrisy. And this makes another juicy tidbit for the press conference—the State Department tried to gag me. Classical blunder number two, Howell."

Howell said nothing. He looked as if he were considering the advisability of wringing his hands.

"I shall inform the press conference of the indecision, reluctance, inaction, incompetence and plain running-scared vacillation of a State Department which will be responsible for the loss of a hundred-million-dollar oil rig, the stopping of cheap supplies of fuel to the American people, the biggest oil slick in history, and the possible—no, I would say probable—beginnings of a third major war. In addition to holding this news conference, I shall buy TV and radio time, explain the whole situation, and further explain that I am forced to go to those extraordinary lengths because of the refusal and inability of the State Department to protect me." He paused. "That was rather silly of me. I have my own TV and radio stations. It's going to be such a burning-hot topic that the big three companies will jump at it and it won't cost me a cent. By tonight I'll have the name of the State Department, particularly the names of you and your boss, if not exactly blackened, at least tarnished across the country. I'm a desperate man, gentlemen, and I'm prepared to adopt desperate methods."

He paused for their reactions. Facially they were all he could have wished. Howell, his assistant and the general all too clearly realized that Lord Worth meant every word he said. The implications were too horrendous to contemplate. But no one said anything, so Lord Worth took up the conversational burden again.

"Finally, gentlemen, you base your pusillanimous refusal to act on the fact that I have no proof of evil intent. I do, in fact, possess such proof, and it's cast iron. I will not lay this proof before you because it is apparent that I will achieve nothing here. I require a decision-maker, and the Secretary has the reputation for being just that. I suggest you get him here."

"*Get* the Secretary?" Howell's ears were clearly appalled by this suggested *lèse majesté*. "One doesn't 'get' the Secretary. People make appointments days, even weeks, in advance. Besides, he is in a very important conference."

Lord Worth remained unmoved. "Get him. This conference he'd better have with me will be the most important of his life. If he elects not to come, then he's probably holding the last conference of his political career. I know he's not twenty yards from here. Get him."

"I—I don't really think—"

Lord Worth rose. "I hope your immediate successors—and the operative word is 'immediate'—will, for the country's sake, display more common sense and intestinal fortitude than you have. Tell the man who, through your gross negligence and cowardly refusal to face facts, will be held primarily responsible for the outbreak of the next war, to watch TV tonight. You have had your chance—as your stenographer's notebook will show—and you've thrown it away." Lord Worth shook his head, almost in sadness. "There are none so blind as those who will not see—especially a spluttering fuse leading to a keg of dynamite. I bid you good day, gentlemen."

"No! No!" Howell was in a state of very considerable agitation. "Sit down! Sit down! I'll see what I can do."

He practically ran from the room.

During his rather protracted absence—he was gone for exactly thirteen minutes—conversation in the room was minimal.

Zweicker said: "You really mean what you say, don't you?"

"Do you doubt me, General?"

"Not any more. You really intend to carry out those threats?"

"I think the word you want is 'promises.' "

After this effective conversation-stopper an uncomfortable silence fell on the room. Only Lord Worth appeared in no way discomforted. He was, or appeared to be, calm and relaxed, which was quite a feat, because he knew that the appearance or nonappearance of the Secretary meant whether he had won or lost.

He'd won. The Secretary, John Benton, when Howell nervously ushered him in, didn't look at all like his reputation—which was that of a tough, shrewd-minded, hard-nosed negotiator, ruthless when the situation demanded and not much given to consulting his cabinet colleagues when it came to decision-making. He looked like a prosperous farmer and exuded warmth and geniality—which deceived Lord Worth, a man who specialized in warmth and geniality not a whit. Here, indeed, was a very different kettle of fish from Howell, a man worthy of Lord Worth's mettle. Lord Worth rose.

Benton shook his hand warmly. "Lord Worth! This is a rare privilege—to have, if I may be forgiven the unoriginal turn of speech, to have America's top oil tycoon calling on us."

Lord Worth was courteous but not deferential. "I wish it were under happier circumstances. My pleasure, Mr. Secretary. It's most kind of you to spare a few moments. Well, five minutes, no more. My promise."

"Take as long as you like." Benton smiled. "You have the reputation for not bandying words. I happen to share that sentiment."

"Thank you." He looked at Howell. "Thirteen minutes to cover forty yards." He looked back at the Secretary. "Mr. Howell will have—ah—apprised you of the situation?"

"I have been fairly well briefed. What do you require of us?" Lord Worth refrained from beaming: here was a man after his own heart. John Benton continued: "We can, of course, approach the Soviet and Venezuelan ambassadors, but that's like approaching a pair of powderpuffs. All they can do is report our suspicions and veiled threats to their respective governments. They're powerless, really. Even ten years ago ambassadors carried weight. They could negotiate and make decisions. Not any more. They have become, through no fault of their own, faceless and empty people who are consistently bypassed in state-to-state negotiations. Even their second chauffeurs, who are customarily trained espionage agents, wield vastly more power than the ambassadors themselves.

"Alternatively, we can make a direct approach to the governments concerned. But for that we would have to have proof. Your word doesn't come into question, but it's not enough. We must be able to adduce positive proof of, shall we say, nefarious intent."

Lord Worth replied immediately. "Such proof I can adduce and can give you the outline now. I am extremely reluctant to name names because it will mean the end of a professional career of a friend of mine. But if I have to, that I will do. Whether I release those names to you or to the public will depend entirely upon the department's reaction. If I can't receive a promise of action after I have given you this outline, then I have no recourse other than to approach the public. This is not blackmail. I'm in a corner and the only solution is to fight my way out of it. If you will, as I hope you will, give me a favorable reaction, I shall, of course, give you a list of names, which, I would hope, will not be published by your department. Secrecy, in other words. Not, of course, that this will prevent you from letting loose the FBI the moment I board my helicopter out there."

"The great warm heart of the American public versus the incompetent bumbling of the State Department." Benton smiled. "One begins to understand why you are a millionaire—I do apologize, billionaire."

"Earlier this week a highly secret meeting was held in a lakeside resort out west. Ten people, all of them very senior oilmen, attended this meeting. Four were Americans, representing many of the major oil companies in the States. A fifth was from Honduras. A sixth was from Venezuela, a seventh from Nigeria. Numbers eight and nine were oil sheikhs from the Gulf. The last was from the Soviet Union. As he was the only one there who had no interest whatsoever in the flow of oil into the United States, one can only presume that he was there to stir up as much trouble as possible."

Lord Worth looked around at the five people

in the room. That he had their collective ear was beyond dispute. Satisfied, he continued.

"The meeting had one purpose and one only in mind. To stop me and to stop me at all costs. More precisely, they wanted to stop the flow of oil from the *Seawitch*—that is the name of my oil rig—because I was considerably undercutting them in price and thereby raising all sorts of fiscal problems. If there are any rules or ethics in the oil business I have as yet to detect any. I believe your congressional investigative committees agree one hundred per cent with me on that. Incidentally, North Hudson—that's the official name of my company—has never been investigated.

"The only permanent way to stop the flow of oil is to destroy the *Seawitch*. Halfway through the meeting they called in a professional trouble-shooter, a man whom I know well, and a highly dangerous man at that. For reasons I won't explain until I get some sort of guarantee of help, he has a deep and bitter grudge against me. He also happens—just coincidentally, of course—to be one of the world's top experts, if not the very top, on the use of high explosives.

"After the meeting this troubleshooter called aside the Venezuelan and Soviet delegates and asked for naval cooperation. This he was guaranteed." Lord Worth looked at the company with a singular lack of enthusiasm. "Now perhaps you people will believe me.

"I would add that this man so hates me that he would probably do the job for nothing. However, he has asked for—and got—a fee of a million dollars. He also asked for—and got— ten million dollars' 'operating expenses.' What does ten million dollars mean to you—except the unlimited use of violence?"

"Preposterous! Incredible!" The Secretary shook his head. "It has, of course, to be true. You are singularly well-informed, Lord Worth. You would appear to have an intelligence service to rival our own."

"Better. I pay them more. This oil business is a jungle and it's a case of survival of the most devious."

"Industrial espionage?"

"Most certainly not." It was just possible that Lord Worth actually believed this.

"This friend who may be coming to the end of his—"

"Yes."

"Give me all the details, including a list of the names. Put a cross against the name of your friend. I shall see to it that he is not implicated and that only I will see that list."

"You are very considerate, Mr. Secretary."

"In return I shall consult with Defense and the Pentagon." He paused. "Even that will not be necessary. In return I can personally guarantee you a sufficiency of air and sea cover against any normal or even considerable hazard."

Lord Worth didn't doubt him. Benton had the reputation of being a man of unshakable integrity. More important, he had the justly deserved reputation of being the President's indispensable right-hand man. Benton delivered. Lord Worth decided against showing too much relief.

"I cannot tell you how deeply grateful I am." He looked at the stenographer and then at Howell. "If I could borrow this lady's services—"

"Of course." The stenographer turned a fresh page in her notebook and waited expectantly.

Lord Worth said: "The place—Lake Tahoe, California. The address—"

The telephone jangled. The stenographer gave Lord Worth an "excuse me" smile and picked up the handset. Howell said to the Secretary: "Dammit, I gave the strictest instructions—"

"It's for Lord Worth." She was looking at Benton. "A Mr. Mitchell from Florida. Extremely urgent." The Secretary nodded and the stenographer rose and handed the phone to Lord Worth.

"Michael? How did you know I was here . . . Yes, I'm listening."

He listened without interruption. As he did so, to the considerable consternation of those watching him, the color drained from his tanned cheeks and left them an unhealthy sallow color. It was Benton himself who rose, poured out a brandy and brought it across to Lord Worth, who took it blindly and drained the not inconsiderable contents at a gulp. Benton took the glass from him and went for a refill. When he came back Lord Worth took the drink but left it untouched. Instead he handed the instrument to Benton and held his left hand over his now screwed-shut eyes.

Benton spoke into the phone. "State Department. Who's speaking?"

Mitchell's voice was faint but clear. "Michael Mitchell, from Lord Worth's home. Is that—is that Dr. Benton?"

"Yes. Lord Worth seems to have received a severe shock."

"Yes, sir. His two daughters have been kidnaped."

"Good God above!" Benton's habitual imperturbability had received a severe dent. No one had even seen him register shock before. Perhaps it was the bluntness of the announcement. "Are you sure?"

"I wish to hell I wasn't, sir."

"Who are you?"

"We—my partner John Roomer and I—are private investigators. We are not here in an investigative capacity. We are here because we are neighbors and friends of Lord Worth and his daughters."

"Called the police?"

"Yes."

"What's been done?"

"We have arranged for the blocking of all air and sea escape routes."

"You have descriptions?"

"Poor. Five men, heavily armed, wearing stocking masks."

"What's your opinion of the local law?"

"Low."

"I'll call in the FBI."

"Yes, sir. But as the criminals haven't been traced, there's no evidence that they've crossed the state line."

"Hell with state lines and regulations. If I say they're called in, that's it. Hold on. I think Lord Worth would like another word." Lord Worth took the receiver. Some color had returned to his cheeks.

"I'm leaving now. Less than three hours, I should say. I'll radio from the Boeing half an hour out. Meet me at the airport."

"Yes, sir. Commander Larsen would like to know—"

"Tell him." Lord Worth replaced the phone, took another sip of his brandy. "There's no fool like an old fool, and only a blind fool would have overlooked so obvious a move. This is war, even if undeclared war, and in war no holds are barred. To think that it should come to this before you had incontrovertible proof that I am indeed under siege. Unforgivable. To have left my daughters unguarded was wholly unforgivable. Why didn't I have the sense to leave Mitchell and Roomer on guard?" He looked at his now-empty glass and the stenographer took it away.

Benton was faintly skeptical. "But against *five* armed men?"

Lord Worth looked at him morosely. "I had forgotten that you don't know those men. Mitchell, for example, could have taken care of them all by himself. He's lethal."

"So they're your friends, and you respect them. Don't take offense, Lord Worth, but is there any way that they could be implicated in this?"

"You must be out of your mind." Lord Worth, still morose, sipped his third brandy. "Sorry, I'm not myself. Sure, they'd like to kidnap my daughters, almost as much as my daughters would like to be kidnaped by them."

"That the way it is?" Benton seemed mildly astonished. In his experience, billionaires' daughters did not normally associate with the likes of private investigators.

"That's the way. And in answer to your next two questions: yes, I approve and no, they don't give a damn about my money." He shook his head wonderingly. "It is extremely odd. And I shall forecast this, Mr. Secretary. When Marina and Melinda are brought back to me it won't be through the good offices of either the local police or your precious FBI. Mitchell and Roomer will bring them back. One does not wish to sound overly dramatic, but they would, quite literally, give their lives for my daughters."

"And, as a corollary, they would cut down anyone who got in their way?"

For the first time since the phone call Lord Worth smiled, albeit faintly. "I'll take the fifth amendment on that one."

"I must meet those paragons sometime."

"Just as long as it's not over the wrong end of Mitchell's gun." He rose, leaving his drink unfinished, and looked round the room. "I must go. Thank you all for your kindness and consideration, not to say forbearance." He left with the Secretary by his side.

When the door closed behind him General Zweicker rose and poured himself a brandy. "Well. What may be the kidnaping of the century pales into insignificance compared to the likelihood of the Russkies starting to throw things at us." He took some brandy. "Don't tell me I'm the only person who can see the hellish witches' brew Lord Worth is stirring up for us?"

It was clear that all three listening to him had a very sharp view of the cauldron. Howell said: "Let's give Lord Worth his due. He could even be right when he says he's glad he's got a British passport. The stirrers-up are our own compatriots; the holier-than-thou major American oil companies, who are willing to crucify Lord Worth and put their country at jeopardy because of their blind stupidity."

"I don't care who's responsible." The stenographer's voice was plaintive. "Does anyone know where I can get a bomb shelter cheap?"

Benton led Worth down one flight of stairs and out onto the sunlit lawn, where the helicopter was waiting.

Benton said: "Ever tried to find words to tell someone how damnably sorry you feel?"

"I know from experience. Don't try. But thanks."

"I could have our personal physician accompany you down to Florida."

"Thanks again. But I'm fine now."

"And you haven't had lunch?" Benton, clearly, was finding conversational gambits heavy going.

"As I don't much care for plastic lunches from plastic trays, I have an excellent French chef aboard my plane." Again a faint smile. "And two stewardesses, chosen solely for their good looks. I shall not want. "

They reached the steps of the helicopter. Benton said: "You've had neither the time nor opportunity to give me that list of names. For the moment that's of no consequence. I just want you to know that my guarantee of protection remains in force."

Lord Worth shook his hand silently and climbed the steps.

By this time Conde, aboard the *Roamer*, had arrived at the *Seawitch*, and the big derrick crane aboard the platform was unloading the heavy weaponry and mines from the Louisiana arsenal. It was a slow and difficult task, for the tip of the derrick boom was two hundred feet above sea level and, in all, the transfer was to take about three hours. As each dual-purpose antiaircraft gun came aboard Larsen selected its site and supervised Palermo and some of his men in securing it in position: this was done by drilling holes in the concrete platform, then anchoring the gun-carriage base with sledgehammer-driven steel spikes. The guns were supposed to be recoilless, but then neither Larsen nor Palermo was much given to taking chances.

The depth charges, when they came, were stacked together in three groups, each halfway between the three apexes of the triangle. That there was an inherent risk in this Larsen was well aware: a stray bullet or shell—or perhaps not so stray—could well trigger the detonating mechanism of one of the depth charges, which would inevitably send up the other charges in sympathetic detonation. But it was a risk that had to be taken if for no other reason than the fact there was no other place where they could be stored ready for immediate use. And when and if the time came for their use the need would be immediate.

The drilling crew watched Palermo and his men at work, their expressions ranging from disinterest to approval. Neither group of men spoke to the other. Larsen was no great believer in fraternization.

Things were going well. The defensive system was being steadily installed. The Christmas tree, the peculiar name given to the valve which controlled the flow of oil from the already tapped reservoir, was wide open and oil was being steadily pumped to the huge storage tank while the derrick drill, set at its widest angle, was driving even deeper into the substratum of the ocean floor, seeking to discover as yet untapped oil deposits. All was going well, there were no overt signs of attack or preparation for attack from air or sea, but Larsen was not as happy as he might have been, even despite the fact that they were still receiving the half-hour regular "on course, on time" reports from the *Torbello*.

He was unhappy partly because of the non-existence of the *Tiburon*. He had recently learned from Galveston that there was no vessel listed in naval or coast guard registries under the name *Tiburon*. He had then asked that they check civilian registrations and had been told that this was a forlorn hope. It would take many hours, perhaps days, to carry out this type of investigation, and private vessels, unless fully insured, would show up neither in official registries nor in those of the major marine-insurance companies. There was no law which said they had to be insured, and the owners of the older and more decrepit craft didn't even bother to insure: there are such things as tax write-offs.

Larsen was not to know that his quest was a hopeless one. When Mulhooney had first taken over the *Tiburon* it had been called the *Hammond,* which he had thoughtfully had painted out and replaced by the name *Tiburon* on the way to Galveston. Since Cronkite had since replaced that by the name *Georgia,* both the *Hammond* and the *Tiburon* had ceased to exist.

But what concerned Larsen even more was his conviction that something was far wrong. He was unable to put a finger on what this might be. He was essentially a pragmatist of the first order, but he was also a man who relied heavily on instinct and intuition. He was a man occasionally given to powerful premonitions, and more often than not those premonitions had turned into reality. And so when the loudspeaker boomed "Commander Larsen to the radio cabin, Commander Larsen to the radio cabin," he was possessed of an immediate certainty that the hour of his premonition had come.

He walked leisurely enough toward the radio cabin, partly because it would never do for Commander Larsen to be seen hurrying anxiously anywhere, partly because he was in no great hurry to hear the bad news he was convinced he was about to hear. He told the radio operator that he would like to take this call privately, waited until the man had left and closed the door behind him, then picked up the telephone.

"Commander Larsen."

"Mitchell. I promised I'd call."

"Thanks. Heard from Lord Worth? He said he'd keep in touch, but no word."

"No wonder. His daughters have been kidnaped."

Larsen said nothing immediately. Judging from the ivoried knuckles, the telephone handpiece seemed in danger of being crushed. Although caring basically only for himself, he had formed an avuncular attachment toward Lord Worth's daughters, but even that was unimportant compared to the implications the kidnaping held for the welfare of the *Seawitch*. When he did speak it was in a steady, controlled voice.

"When did this happen?"

"This morning. And no trace of them. We've blocked every escape route in the southern part of the state. And there is no report from any port or airport of any unusual departure since the time of the kidnaping."

"Vanished into thin air?"

"Vanished, anyway. But not into thin air, we think. Terra firma, more likely. We think they've gone to earth, and are holed up not far away. But it's only a guess."

"No communication, no demands, from the kidnapers?"

"None. That's what makes it all so odd."

"You think this is a ransom kidnap?"

"No."

"The *Seawitch?*"

"Yes."

"Do you know why Lord Worth went to Washington?"

"No. I'd like to."

"To demand naval protection. Early this morning a Russian destroyer and a Cuban submarine left Havana, while another destroyer left Venezuela. They are on converging courses. The point of convergence would appear to be the *Seawitch*."

There was a silence, then Mitchell said: "This is for sure?"

"Yes. Well, Lord Worth's cup of woes would seem to be fairly full. The only consolation is that nothing much else can happen to him after this. Please keep me informed."

In Lord Worth's radio room both Mitchell and Roomer hung up their phones.

Mitchell briefly indulged in some improper language. "God, I never thought his enemies would go to this length."

Roomer said: "Neither did I. I'm not sure that I even think so now."

"You mean Uncle Sam's not going to let any foreign naval powers play games in our own backyard?"

"Something like that. I don't think the Soviets

would go so far as to risk a confrontation. Could be a bluff, a diversionary move. Maybe the real attack is coming from elsewhere."

"Maybe anything. Could be a double bluff. One thing's sure: Larsen's right in saying that Lord Worth's cup of woes is fairly full. In fact, I'd say it was running over."

"Looks that way," Roomer said absently. His thoughts were clearly elsewhere.

Mitchell said: "Don't tell me you're in the throes of intuition again?"

"I'm not sure. When you were talking to Larsen just now you mentioned 'terra firma.' Firm land, dry land. What if it weren't dry land? What if it were *un*firm land?"

Mitchell waited patiently.

Roomer said: "If you wanted to hole up, really get lost in Florida, where would you go?"

Mitchell hardly had to think. "You're right! Unfirm land, infirm land, whatever you want to call it. The Everglades, of course. Where else?"

"Man could hide out for a month there, and a battalion of troops couldn't find him. Which explains why the cops have been unable to find the station wagon." Between them, MacPherson and Jenkins had been able to give a fairly accurate description of the kidnapers' wagon. "They've been checking the highways and byways. I'll bet they never even thought of checking the roads into the swamps."

"Did we?"

"Right. We blew it. There are dozens of those roads into the glades, but most of them are very short and right away you reach a point where a wheeled vehicle can't go any further. A few dozen police cars could comb the nearest swamps in an hour."

Mitchell said to Robertson: "Get Chief McGarrity."

A knock came on the half-open door and Louise, one of the young housemaids, entered. She held a card in her hand. She said: "I was just making up Miss Marina's bed when I found this between the sheets."

Mitchell took the card. It was a plain calling card giving Marina's name and address.

Louise said: "Other side."

Mitchell reversed the card, holding it so that Roomer could see. Handwritten with a ballpoint were the words: "Vacation. Little island in the sun. No swimsuit."

"You know Marina's handwriting, Louise?" Mitchell had suddenly realized that he didn't.

The girl looked at the card. "Yes, sir. I'm sure."

"Thanks, Louise. This could be very useful." Louise smiled and left. Mitchell said to Roomer: "What kind of lousy detective are you? Why didn't *you* think of searching the bedrooms?"

"Hmm. She must have asked them to leave while she dressed."

"You'd have thought she'd have been too scared to think of this."

"The handwriting's steady enough. Besides, she doesn't scare easily. Except, that is, when you point a gun between her eyes."

"I wish, right here and now, that I was pointing a gun between someone else's eyes. Little island in the sun where you can't go bathing. An overconfident kidnaper can talk too much. You thinking what I'm thinking?"

Roomer nodded. "The *Seawitch*."

At thirty-three thousand feet, Lord Worth had just completed a light but delicious lunch accompanied by a splendid Bordeaux wine, specially laid down for him in a Rothschild winery. He had regained his habitual calm. He had, he reckoned, touched his nadir. All that could happen had happened. In common with Larsen, Mitchell and Roomer, he was convinced that the fates could touch him no more. All four were completely and terribly wrong. The worst was yet to come. It was, in fact, happening right then.

Colonel Farquharson, Lieutenant-Colonel Dewings, and Major Breckley were not in fact the people their ID cards claimed they were, for the sufficient reason that there were no officers of that rank with corresponding names in the U. S. Army. But then, it was a very big army, and nobody, not even the officers, could possibly be expected to know the names of more than a tiny fraction of their fellow officers. Nor were their faces their normal faces, although they could hardly be described as being heavily disguised. The man responsible had been a Hollywood make-up artist who preferred subtlety to false beards. All three men were dressed in sober and well-cut business suits.

Farquharson presented his card to the corporal at the outer reception desk. "Colonel Farquharson to see Colonel Pryce."

"I'm afraid he's not here, sir."

"Then the officer in charge, soldier."

"Yes, sir."

A minute later they were seated before a young and apprehensive Captain Martin, who had just finished a rather reluctant and very perfunctory scrutiny of the ID cards.

Farquharson said: "So Colonel Pryce has been called to Washington. I can guess why."

He didn't have to guess. He himself had put through the fake call that had led to Pryce's abrupt departure. "And his second in command?"

"Flu, sir." Martin sounded apologetic.

"At this time of year? How inconvenient. Especially today. You can guess why we're here."

"Yes, sir." Martin looked slightly unhappy. "Security check. I had a phone call telling me of the break-ins into the Florida and Louisiana depots." Dewings had put through that one. "I'm sure you'll find everything in order, sir."

"Doubtless. I have already discovered something that is not in order."

"Sir?" There was a definite apprehension now in Martin's voice and appearance.

"Security-consciousness. Do you know that there are literally dozens of shops where I could buy, perfectly legally, a general's uniform. Those are the specialty shops that cater primarily to the film and stage industries. If I walked in dressed in such a uniform, would you accept me for what my uniform proclaimed me to be?"

"I suppose I would, sir."

"Well, don't. Not ever again." He glanced at his identity card lying on the desk. "Forging one of those presents no problems. When a stranger makes an appearance in a top security place like this, always, *always,* check his identity with Area Command. And always talk only to the commanding officer."

"Yes, sir. Do you happen to know his name? I'm new here."

"Major-General Harsworth."

Martin had the corporal at the front desk put him through. On the first ring a voice answered. "Area Command."

The voice did not in fact come from Area Command. It came from a man less than half a mile away, seated at the base of a telephone pole. He had with him a battery-powered transceiver. An insulated copper line from that led up to an alligator clip attached to one of the telephone wires.

Martin said: "Netley Rowan Arsenal. Captain Martin. I'd like to speak to General Harsworth."

"Hold on, please." There was a series of clicks, a pause of some seconds, then the same voice said: "On the line, Captain."

Martin said: "General Harsworth."

"Speaking." The man by the telephone pole had deepened his voice by an octave. "Problems, Captain Martin?"

"I have Colonel Farquharson with me. He insists that I check out his identity with you."

The voice at the other end was sympathetic. "Been getting a security lecture?"

"I'm afraid I have, sir."

"The colonel's very hot on security. He's with Lieutenant-Colonel Dewings and Major Breckley?"

"Yes, sir."

"Well, it's hardly the end of your professional career. But he's right, you know."

Farquharson himself took the wheel of the car on the three-mile journey, a chastened, compliant Martin sitting up front beside him. A fifteen-foot-high electrical-warning barbed-wire fence surrounded the arsenal, a squat, gray, windowless building covering almost half an acre of land. A sentry with a machine carbine barred the entrance to the compound. He recognized Captain

Martin, stepped back and saluted. Farquharson drove up to the one and only door of the building and halted. The four men got out. Farquharson said to Martin: "Major Breckley has never been inside a TNW installation before. A few illuminating comments, perhaps?" It would be illuminating for Farquharson also. He had never been inside an arsenal of any description in his life.

"Yes, sir. TNW—Tactical Nuclear Warfare. Walls thirty-three inches thick, alternating steel and ferroconcrete. Door ten inches tungsten steels. Both walls and door capable of resisting the equivalent of a fourteen-inch armor-piercing naval shell. This glass panel is recording us on TV videotape. This meshed grill is a two-way speaker which also records our voices." He pressed a button sunk in the concrete.

A voice came through the grill. "Identification, please?"

"Captain Martin with Colonel Farquharson and security inspection."

"Code?"

"Geronimo." The massive door began to slide open and they could hear the hum of a powerful electrical motor. It took all of ten seconds for the door to open to its fullest extent. Martin led them inside.

A corporal saluted their entrance. Martin said: "Security inspection tour."

"Yes, sir." The corporal didn't seem too happy.

Farquharson said: "You worried about something, soldier?"

"No, sir."

"Then you should be."

Martin said: "Something wrong, sir?" He was patently nervous.

"Four things." Martin dipped his head so that Farquharson couldn't see his nervous swallowing. One thing would have been bad enough.

"In the first place, that sentry gate should be kept permanently locked. It should only be opened after a phone call to your HQ and an electronic link for opening the gate installed in your office. What's to prevent a person or persons with a silenced automatic disposing of your sentry and driving straight up here? Second, what would prevent people walking through the open doorway and spraying us all with submachine guns? That door should have been shut the moment we passed through." The corporal started to move but Farquharson stopped him with upraised hand.

"Third, all people who are not base personnel—such as we—should be fingerprinted on arrival. I will arrange to have your guards trained in those techniques. Fourth, and most important, show me the controls for those doors."

"This way, sir." The corporal led the way to a small console. "The red button opens, the green one closes."

Farquharson pressed the green button. The

massive door hissed slowly closed. "Unsatisfactory. Totally. Those are the only controls to operate the door?"

"Yes, sir." Martin looked very unhappy indeed.

"We shall have another electronic link established with your HQ, which will render those buttons inoperable until the correct signal is sent." Farquharson was showing signs of irritation. "I would have thought all those things were self-evident."

Martin smiled weakly. "They are now, sir."

"What percentage of explosives, bombs and shells stored here are conventional?"

"Close to ninety-five per cent, sir."

"I'd like to see the nuclear weapons first."

"Of course, sir." A now thoroughly demoralized Martin led the way.

The TNW section was compartmented off but not sealed. One side was lined with what appeared to be shells, stowed on racks; the other, with pear-shaped metal canisters about thirty inches high, with buttons, a clockface and a large knurled screw on top. Beyond them were stacked suitcases, each with two leather handles.

Breckley indicated the pear-shaped canisters. "What are those? Bombs?"

"Both bombs and land mines." Martin seemed glad to talk and take his mind off his troubles. "Those controls on top are relatively simple. Before you get at those two red switches you have to unscrew those two transparent plastic covers. The switches have then to be turned ninety degrees to the right. They are then still in the safe position. They then have to be flipped ninety degrees to the left. This is the ready-to-activate position.

"Before that is done, you have to put the time setting on the clock. That is done by means of this knurled knob here. One complete turn means a one-minute time delay which will show up on this clockface here. It registers in seconds, as you can see. Total time delay is thirty minutes—thirty turns."

"And this black button?"

"The most important of them all. No cover and no turning. You might want to get at it in a hurry. Depressing that stops the clock and, in fact, deactivates the bomb."

"What's the area of damage?"

"Compared to the conventional atom bomb, tiny. The vaporization area would be a quarter-mile radius. Perhaps less. The blast, shock and radiation areas would, of course, be considerably greater."

"You mean they can be used as both bombs and mines?"

"Instead of mines, maybe I should have said an explosive device for use on land. As bombs the setting would probably be only six seconds—in tactical warfare they would be carried by low-flying supersonic planes. They'd be about two miles clear by the time the bomb went off and moving too fast for the shock waves to catch up with them. For land use—well, say you wanted to infiltrate an ammunition dump. You'd check how long it would take you to infiltrate there, calculate how long it would take you to get out and clear of the blast zone, and set the timer accordingly.

"The missiles here—"

"We've seen and heard enough," Farquharson said. "Kindly put your hands up."

Five minutes later, with the furiously reluctant assistance of Martin, they had loaded two of the bombs, safely concealed in their carrying cases, into the trunk of their car. In the process the purpose of the two carrying handles became clear: each bomb must have weighed at least ninety pounds.

Farquharson went back inside, looked indifferently at the two bound men, pressed the button and slipped through the doorway as the door began to close. He waited until the door was completely shut, then climbed into the front seat beside Martin, who was at the wheel this time. Farquharson said: "Remember, one false move and you're a dead man. We will, of course, have to kill the sentry too."

There were no false moves. About a mile from the building the car stopped by a thicket of stunted trees. Martin was marched deep into the thicket, bound, gagged and attached to a tree just in case he might have any ideas about jack-knifing his way down to the roadside. Farquharson looked down at him.

"Your security *was* lousy. We'll phone your HQ in an hour or so, let them know where they can find you. I trust there are not too many rattlesnakes around."

Chapter 6

ROBERTSON looked up from the radio console. "Chief McGarrity."

Mitchell took the phone. "Mitchell? We've found the kidnapers' estate wagon. Down by the Wyanee Swamp." McGarrity sounded positively elated. "I'm going there personally. Tracker dogs. I'll wait for you at the Walnut Tree crossing." Mitchell replaced the receiver and said to Roomer: "McGarrity's got it all wrapped up. He's found the estate wagon. Well . . . *someone* did, but of course it will be made clear eventually that it was McGarrity."

"Empty, of course. Doesn't that old fool know

that this makes it more difficult, not easier? At least we knew what transport they were using. Not any more. He didn't mention anything about bringing along a newspaper photographer that he just sort of accidentally bumped into?"

"Tracker dogs were all he mentioned."

"Did he suggest anything for the dogs to sniff at?" Mitchell shook his head, Roomer shook his and called to Jenkins. "Will you get Louise, please?"

Louise appeared very quickly. Roomer said: "We need a piece of clothing that the ladies used to wear a lot."

She looked uncertain. "I don't understand—"

"Some things we can give bloodhounds to sniff so that they pick up their scent."

"Oh." It required only a second's thought. "Their dressing gowns, of course." This with but the slightest hint of disapproval, as if the girls spent most of the day lounging about in those garments.

"Handle as little as possible, please. Put each in a separate plastic bag."

A patrol car and a small closed police van awaited them at the Walnut Tree crossing. McGarrity was standing by the police car. He was a small bouncy man who radiated goodwill and only stopped smiling when he was vehemently denouncing corruption in politics. He was a police chief of incomparable incompetence, but was a consummate and wholly corrupt politician, which was why he was police chief. He shook the hands of Mitchell and Roomer with all the warmth and sincerity of an incumbent coming up for re-election, which was precisely what he was.

. "Glad to meet you two gentlemen at last. Heard very good reports about you." He appeared to have conveniently forgotten his allegation that they gave a lot of trouble to the local law. "Appreciate all the co-operation you've given me—and for turning up here now. This is Ron Stewart of the *Herald*." He gestured through an open car window where a man, apparently festooned in cameras, sat in the back seat. "Kind of accidentally bumped into him."

Mitchell choked, turning it into a cough. "Too many cigarettes."

"Same failing myself. Driver's the dog handler. Driver of the van is the other one. Just follow us, please."

Five miles farther on they reached the turn-off—one of many—into the Wyanee Swamp. The foliage of the trees, almost touching overhead, quickly reduced the light to that of a late winter afternoon. The increase in the humidity was almost immediately noticeable, as was the sour, nose-wrinkling miasma as they neared the swamp. A distinctly unhealthy atmosphere, or such was the first impression: but many people with a marked aversion to what passed for civilization lived there all their lives and seemed none the worse for it.

The increasingly rutted, bumpy road had become almost intolerable until they rounded a blind corner and came across the abandoned station wagon.

The first essential was, apparently, that pictures be taken, and the second that McGarrity be well-placed in each one, his hand preferably resting in a proprietorial fashion on the hood. That done, the cameraman fitted a flash attachment and was reaching for the rear door when Roomer clamped his wrist not too gently. "Don't do that!"

"Why not?"

"Never been on a criminal case before? Fingerprints is why not." He looked at McGarrity. "Expecting them soon?"

"Shouldn't be long. Out on a case. Check on them, Don." This to the driver, who immediately got busy on his radio. It was clear that the idea of bringing fingerprint experts along had never occurred to McGarrity.

The dogs were released from the van. Roomer and Mitchell opened up their plastic bags and allowed the dogs to sniff the dressing gowns. McGarrity said: "What you got there?"

"The girls' dressing gowns. To give your hounds a scent. We knew you'd want something."

"Of course. But dressing gowns!" McGarrity was a past master in covering up. Something else, clearly, that had not occurred to him.

The dogs caught the scents at once and strained at their leashes as they nosed their way down a rutted path, for the road had come to an abrupt end. Inside a hundred yards, their path was blocked by water. It wasn't a true part of the swamp but a slow, meandering, mud-brown creek, perhaps twenty feet across, if that. There was a mooring post nearby, with a similar one at the far bank. Also by the far bank was a warped and aged craft which not even the charitable could have called a boat. It was built along the lines of an oversized coffin, with a squared-off end where the bow should have been. The ferry—probably the most kindly name for it— was attached to the two posts by an endless pulley line.

The two dog handlers hauled the boat across, got into it with understandable caution, and were joined by their dogs, who kept on displaying considerable signs of animation, an animation which rapidly diminished, then vanished shortly after they had landed on the far bank. After making a few fruitless circles, they lay down dejectedly on the ground.

"Well, ain't that a shame," a voice said. "Trail gone cold, I guess."

The four men on the near bank turned to look at the source of the voice. He was a bizarre character, wearing a new panama hat with a tartan band, gleaming thigh-length leather boots (presumably as a protection against snakebites), and clothes discarded by a scarecrow. "You folks chasin' someone?"

"We're looking for someone," McGarrity said cautiously.

"Lawmen, yes?"

"Chief of Police McGarrity."

"Honored, I'm sure. Well, Chief, you're wasting your time. Hot trail here, cold on the other side. So the party you're looking for got off halfway across."

"You saw them?" McGarrity asked suspiciously.

"Hah! More than one, eh? No, sir. Just happened by right now. But if I was on the run from the law that's what I'd do, because it's been done hundreds of times. You can get out midway, walk half a mile, even a mile, upstream or downstream. Dozens of little rivulets come into this creek. You could turn up any of those, go a mile into the swamp without setting foot on dry land. Wouldn't find them this side of Christmas, Chief."

"How deep is the creek?"

"Fifteen inches. If that."

"Then, why the boat? I mean, with those boots you could walk across without getting your feet wet."

The stranger looked almost shocked. "No sirree. Takes me an hour every morning to polish up them critters." It was assumed that he was referring to his boots. "Besides, there're the water moccasins." He seemed to have a rooted aversion to snakes. "The boat? Come the rains, the creek's up to here." He touched his chest.

McGarrity called the dog handlers to return. Mitchell said to the stranger: "Anyplace in the swamp where a helicopter could land?"

"Sure. More firm land out there than there is swampland. Never seen any helicopters, though. Yes, lots of clearings."

The dog handlers and dogs disembarked. Leaving the stranger to flick some invisible dust off his boots they made their way back to the station wagon. Mitchell said: "Wait a minute. I've got an idea." He opened the two plastic bags containing the dressing gowns and presented them to the dogs again. He then walked back up the rutted lane, past the two cars and vans, beckoning the dog handlers to follow him, which they did, almost having to drag the reluctant dogs behind them.

After about twenty yards the reluctance vanished. The dogs yelped and strained at their leashes. For another twenty yards they towed their handlers along behind them, then abruptly stopped and circled a few times before sitting down dispiritedly. Mitchell crouched and examined the surface of the lane. The others caught up with him.

McGarritty said: "What gives, then?"

"This." Mitchell pointed to the ground. "There was another vehicle here. You can see where its back wheels spun when it started to reverse. The kidnapers guessed we'd be using dogs—it wasn't all that hard a guess. So they carried the girls twenty yards or so, to break the scent, before setting them down again."

"Right smart of you, Mr. Mitchell, right smart." McGarrity didn't look as pleased as his words suggested. "So the birds have flown, eh? And now we haven't the faintest idea what the getaway vehicle looks like."

Roomer said: "Somebody's flown, that's for sure. But maybe only one or two. Maybe they've gone to borrow a helicopter."

"A helicopter?" The waters didn't have to be very deep for Chief McGarrity to start floundering.

With a trace of weary impatience Mitchell said: "It could be a double bluff. Maybe they reversed the procedure and took the girls back to the station wagon again. Maybe they're still in the swamp, waiting for a helicopter to come and pick them up. You heard the old boy back there—he said there were plenty of places in the swamp where a helicopter could set down."

McGarrity nodded sagely and appeared to ponder the matter deeply. The time had come, he felt, for him to make a positive contribution. "The swamp's out. Hopeless. So I'll have to concentrate on the helicopter angle."

Mitchell said: "How do you propose to do that?"

"Just you leave that to me."

Roomer said: "That's hardly fair, Chief. We've given you our complete confidence. Don't you think we're entitled to some in return?"

"Well, now." McGarrity appeared to ruminate, although he was secretly pleased to be asked the question, as Roomer had known he would be. "If the chopper doesn't get in there, it can't very well lift them out, can it?"

"That's a fact," Roomer said solemnly.

"So I station marksmen round this side of the swamp. It's no big deal to bring down a low-flying chopper."

Mitchell said: "I wouldn't do that if I were you."

"No, indeed." Roomer shook his head. "The law frowns on murder."

"Murder?" McGarrity stared at them. "Who's talking about murder?"

"*We* are," Mitchell said. "Rifle or machine-gun fire could kill someone inside the helicopter. If it brings down the helicopter they'd all probably die. Maybe there are criminals aboard, but they're entitled to a fair trial. And has it occurred to you that the pilot will almost certainly be an innocent party with a pistol pointed at his head?" McGarrity, clearly, had not thought of that. "Not going to make us very popular, is it?"

McGarrity winced. Even the thought of un-popularity and the forthcoming election made him feel weak inside.

"So what the devil do we do?"

Roomer was frank. "I'll be damned if I know. You can post observers. You can even have a grounded helicopter standing by to chase the other one when it takes off. *If* it ever comes in the first place. We're only guessing."

"No more we can do here," Mitchell said. "We've already missed too many appointments today. We'll be in touch."

Back on the highway Roomer said: "How do you think he'd do as a dogcatcher?"

"Place would be overrun by stray dogs in a few months. How much faith have you got in this idea that they might use a helicopter?"

"A lot. If they just wanted to change cars they wouldn't have gone through this elaborate rig-marole. They could have parked their station wagon out of sight almost anyplace. By ap-parently going into hiding in the swamp they wanted to make it look as though they were preparing to hole up in there for some time. They hadn't figured on our backing—your back-tracking—up the lane."

"We're pretty sure their destination is the *Seawitch*. We're pretty sure they'll use a heli-copter. Which helicopter and pilot would you use?"

"Lord Worth's. Not only are his pilots almost certainly the only ones who know the exact co-ordinates of the *Seawitch,* but those distinctly marked North Hudson helicopters are the only ones that could approach the *Seawitch* without raising suspicion." Roomer reached for the phone, fiddled with the wave-band control and raised Lord Worth's house. "Jim?"

"Go ahead, Mr. Roomer."

"We're coming back there. Look for Lord Worth's address book. Probably right by you in your radio room. Make us a list of the names and addresses of his helicopter pilots. Is the gate-keeper at the heliport on the radio-phone, too?"

"Yes."

"Get that for us too, please."

"Roger."

Roomer said to Mitchell: "Still think we shouldn't warn Larsen about our suspicions?"

"That's for sure." Mitchell was very definite. "The *Seawitch* is Larsen's baby, and the kind of reception he'd prepare for them might be a bit overenthusiastic. How'd you like to explain to Lord Worth how come his daughters got caught in the crossfire?"

"No way!" Roomer spoke with some feeling.

"Or even explain to yourself how Melinda got shot through the lung?"

Roomer ignored him. "What if we're wrong about Worth's pilots?"

"Then we turn the whole thing over to that ace detective, McGarrity."

"So we'd better be right."

They were right. They were also too late.

John Campbell was both an avid fisherman and an avid reader. He had long since mastered the techniques of indulging his two pleasures simultaneously. A creek, fairly popular with fish, ran within twenty feet of his back porch. Campbell was sitting on a canvas chair, parasol over his head, alternating every page with a fresh cast of his line, when Durand and one of his men, stocking-masked and holding guns in their hands, came into his line of vision. Campbell rose to his feet, book still in hand.

"Who are you and what do you want?"

"You. You're Campbell, aren't you?"

"What if I am?"

"Like you to do a little job for us."

"What job?"

"Fly a helicopter for us."

"I'll be damned if I will!"

"So you *are* Campbell. Come along."

Following the gesturing of their guns, Campbell moved between the two men. He was within one foot of Durand's gun hand when he chopped the side of his hand on the wrist that held the gun. Durand grunted in pain, the gun fell to the ground and a second later the two men were locked together, wrestling, kicking and punching with a fine disregard for the rules of sport, altering position so frequently that Durand's henchman at first found no opportunity to intervene. But the opportunity came very soon. The unsportsmanlike but effective use of Campbell's right knee doubled Durand over in gasping agony, but enough instinct was left him to seize Campbell's shirt as he fell over backward. This was Campbell's downfall in more ways than one, for the back of his head was now nakedly vulnerable to a swung automatic.

The man who had felled Campbell now pulled him clear, allowing Durand to climb painfully to his feet, although still bent over at an angle of forty-five degrees. He pulled off his stocking mask as if to try to get more air to breathe. Durand was Latin American, with a pale coffee-colored face, thick black curling hair and a pencil-line mustache; he might even qualify as handsome when the twisted lines of agony ceased to contort his face. He straightened inch by inch and finally obtained a modicum of breath—enough, at least, to allow him to announce what he would like to do with Campbell.

"Some other time, Mr. Durand. He can't very well fly a chopper from a hospital bed."

Durand painfully acknowledged the truth of this. "I hope *you* didn't hit him too hard."

"Just a tap."

"Tie him, tape him and blindfold him."

Durand was now a scarce twenty degrees off the vertical. His helper left for the car and returned in moments with cord, tape and blindfold. Three minutes later they were on their way, with a rug-covered and still unconscious Campbell on the floor at the back. Resting comfortably on the rug were Durand's feet—he still didn't feel quite up to driving. Both men had their masks off now—even in the free-wheeling state of Florida men driving with stocking masks on were likely to draw more than passing attention.

Mitchell glanced briefly at the list of names and addresses Robertson had given them. "Fine. But what are these checks opposite five of the names?"

Robertson sounded apologetic. "I hope you don't mind—I don't want to butt in—but I took the liberty of phoning those gentlemen to see if they would be at home when you came around. I assumed you'd be seeing them because you asked for the addresses."

Mitchell looked at Roomer. "Why the hell didn't you think of that?"

Roomer bestowed a cold glance on him and said to Robertson: "Maybe I should have you as a partner. What did you find out?"

"One pilot is standing by at the airport. Four of the others are at home. The one whose name I haven't checked—John Campbell—isn't home.

I asked one of the other pilots about this and he seemed a bit surprised. Said that Campbell usually spends his afternoons fishing outside the back of his house. He's a bachelor and lives in a pretty isolated place."

"It figures," Roomer said. "A bachelor in isolation. The kidnapers seem to have an excellent intelligence system. The fact that he doesn't answer the phone may mean nothing—he could have gone for a walk, shopping, visiting friends. On the other hand—"

"Yes. Especially on the other hand." Mitchell turned to leave, then said to Robertson: "Does the gatekeeper have a listed phone number as well as the radiophone?"

"I've typed it on that list."

"Maybe we should both have you as a partner."

Mitchell and Roomer stood on Campbell's back lawn and surveyed the scene unemotionally. The canvas chair, on its side, had a broken leg. The parasol was upturned on the grass, over an opened book. The fishing rod was in the water up to its handle and would have floated away had not the reel snagged on a shrub root. Roomer retrieved the rod while Mitchell hurried through the back doorway—the back door was wide open, as was the front. He dialed a phone number, and got an answer on the first ring.

"Lord Worth's heliport. Gorrie here."

"My name's Mitchell. You have a police guard?"

"Mr. Mitchell? You Lord Worth's friend?"

"Yes."

"Sergeant Roper is here."

"That all? Let me speak to him." There was hardly a pause before Roper came on the phone.

"Mike? Nice to hear from you again."

"Listen, Sergeant, this is urgent. I'm speaking from the house of John Campbell, one of Lord Worth's pilots. He has been forcibly abducted, almost certainly by some of the kidnapers of Lord Worth's daughters. I have every reason to believe—no time for explanations now—that they're heading in your direction with the intention of hijacking one of Lord Worth's helicopters and forcing Campbell to fly it. There'll be two of them at least, maybe three, armed and dangerous. I suggest you call up reinforcements immediately. If we get them we'll break them— at least Roomer and I will; you can't, you're a law officer and your hands are tied—and we'll find where the girls are and get them back."

"Reinforcements coming up. Then I'll look the other way."

Mitchell hung up. Roomer was by his side. Roomer said: "You prepared to go as far as back-room persuasion to get the information we want?"

Mitchell looked at him bleakly. "I look forward to it. Don't you?"

"No. But I'll go along with you."

Once again Mitchell and Roomer had guessed correctly. And once again they were too late.

Mitchell had driven to Lord Worth's heliport with a minimum regard for traffic and speed regulations, and now, having arrived there, he realized bitterly that his haste had been wholly unnecessary.

Five men greeted their arrival, although it was hardly a cheerful meeting: Gorrie, the gateman, and four policemen. Gorrie and Sergeant Roper were tenderly massaging their wrists. Mitchell looked at Roper.

"Don't tell me." Mitchell sounded weary. "They jumped you before the reinforcements were to hand."

"Yeah." Roper's face was dark with anger. "I know it sounds like the old lame excuse, but we never had a chance. This car comes along and stops outside the gatehouse, right here. The driver—he was alone in the car—seemed to be having a sneezing fit and was holding a big wad of Kleenex to his face."

Roomer said: "So you wouldn't recognize him again?"

"Exactly. Well, we were watching this dude when a voice from the back—the back window was open—told us to freeze. I didn't even have my hand on my gun. We froze. Then he told me to drop my gun. Well, this guy was no more than five feet away . . . I dropped my gun. Dead heroes are no good to anyone. Then he told us to turn around. He was wearing a stocking mask. Then the driver came and tied our wrists behind our backs. When we turned around he was wearing a stocking mask too."

"Then they tied your feet and tied you together so that you wouldn't have any funny ideas about using a telephone?"

"That's how it was. But they weren't worried about the phones. They cut the lines before they took off."

"They took off immediately?"

Gorrie said: "No. Five minutes later. The pilots always radio-file a flight plan before take-off. I suppose these guys forced Campbell to do the same. To make it look kosher."

Mitchell shrugged his indifference. "Means nothing. You can file a flight plan to anyplace. Doesn't mean you have to keep it. How about fuel—for the helicopters, I mean?"

"Fuel's always kept topped up. My job. Lord Worth's orders."

"What direction did they go?"

"Thataway." Gorrie indicated with an outstretched arm.

"Well, the birds have flown. Might as well be on our way."

"Just like that?" Roper registered surprise.

"What do you expect me to do that the police can't?"

"Well, for starters, we could call in the Air Force."

"Why?"

"They could force it down."

Mitchell sighed. "There's a great deal of crap being talked about forcing planes down. What if they refuse to be forced down?"

"Then shoot it down."

"With Lord Worth's daughters aboard? Lord Worth wouldn't be very pleased. Neither would you. Think of all the cops that would be out of a job."

"Lord Worth's daughters!"

"It's all this routine police work," Roomer said. "Atrophies the brain. Who the hell do you think that helicopter has gone to pick up?"

Once clear of the heliport, Roomer extended an arm. " 'Thataway,' the man said. 'Thataway' is northwest. The Wyanee Swamp."

"Even if they'd taken off to the southeast they'd still have finished up in Wyanee." Mitchell pulled up by a public booth. "How are you with McGarrity's voice?" Roomer was an accomplished mimic.

"It's not the voice that's hard. It's the thought processes. I'll give it a try." He didn't say what he was going to try because he didn't have to. He left for the booth and was back inside two minutes.

"Campbell filed a flight plan for the *Seawitch*."

"Any questions asked?"

"Not really. Told them that some fool had made a mistake. Anyone who knows McGarrity would know who the fool was that made the mistake."

Mitchell started the engine, then switched off as the phone rang. Mitchell lifted the receiver.

"Jim here. Tried to ring you a couple of times, fifteen minutes ago, five minutes ago."

"Figures. Out of the car both times. More bad news?"

"Not unless you consider Lord Worth bad news. Touchdown in fifteen minutes."

"We got time."

"Says he's coming up to the house."

"Sent for the Rolls?"

"No. Probably wants to talk private. And it looks as if he's planning to stay away some time. Ordered a bag packed for a week."

"Seven white suits." Mitchell hung up.

Roomer said: "Looks as if we're going to have to do some bag-packing ourselves." Mitchell nodded and started up again.

Lord Worth was looking his old self when he settled in the back seat of their car. Not quite radiating his old bonhomie, to be sure, but calm and lucid and, to all appearances, relaxed. He told of his success in Washington, for which he was duly and politely congratulated. Roomer then told him in detail what had happened in his absence: this time the absence of congratulations was marked.

"You've notified Commander Larsen of your suspicions, of course?"

"Not suspicions," Mitchell said. "Certainties. And there's no 'of course' and no, we didn't notify him. I'm primarily responsible for that."

"Taking the law into your own hands, eh? Mind telling me why?"

"You're the person who knows Larsen best. You know how possessive he is about the *Sea-witch*. You yourself have told us about his anger and violence. Do you think a man like that, duly forewarned, wouldn't have a very warm reception waiting for the kidnapers? Stray bullets, ricocheting bullets, are no respector of persons, Lord Worth. You want a daughter crippled for life? We prefer that the kidnapers establish a bloodless beachhead."

"Well, all right." The words came grudgingly. "But from now on keep me fully informed of your intentions and decisions." Lord Worth, Roomer noted with sardonic amusement, had no intention of dispensing with their unpaid services. "But no more taking the law into your own hands, do you hear?"

Mitchell stopped car and engine. Roomer's amusement changed to apprehension. Mitchell twisted in his seat and looked at Lord Worth in cool speculation.

"You're a fine one to talk."

"What do you mean, sir?" There were fifteen generations of highland aristocracy in the glacial voice.

Mitchell remained unmoved. "For taking the law into your own hands by breaking into and robbing that arsenal last night. If Roomer and I were decent citizens and law-abiding detectives, we'd have had you behind bars last night. Not even a billionaire can get away with that sort of thing, especially when it involves the assault and locking up of the arsenal guards. John and I were there." Mitchell was not above a little prevarication when the need arose.

"*You* were there." Most rarely for him, Lord Worth was at a loss for words. He recovered quickly. "But *I* wasn't there."

"We know that. We also know you sanctioned the break-in. Ordered it, rather."

"Balderdash. And if you actually witnessed this, why did you not stop it?"

"John and I take our chances. But not against nine men armed with machine guns."

This gave Lord Worth pause. They had their figures and facts right. Clearly they had been there. He said: "Supposing any of this rigmarole were true, how in God's name do you tie me up with it?"

"Now you're being a fool. We were also at your heliport. We saw the truck arrive. We saw nine men unload a fairly massive quantity of more than fairly lethal weaponry into one helicopter. Then a man drove the truck away—an army truck, of course—back to the arsenal from where it had been stolen. The other eight men boarded another helicopter. Then a minibus arrived, carrying twelve heavily armed thugs who joined the other eight. John and I recognized no fewer than five of them—two of them we've personally put behind bars." Roomer looked at him admiringly, but Mitchell wasn't looking at Roomer, he was looking at Lord Worth, and both voice and tone were devoid of any form of encouragement. "It came as a shock to both of us to find that Lord Worth was consorting with common criminals. You're sweating a little, Lord Worth. Why are you sweating?"

Lord Worth didn't enlighten them as to why he was sweating.

"And then, of course, you came along in the Rolls. One of the very best sequences we got on our infrared movie camera last night." Roomer blinked, but that Lord Worth believed Mitchell Roomer did not for a moment doubt: everything that Mitchell had said, even the slight embellishments, Lord Worth knew or believed to be true, so he had no reason to doubt the truth of the camera fiction.

"We actually considered phoning the nearest army HQ and having them send along some armored cars and a trailered tank. Even your thugs wouldn't have stood a chance. We thought of going down the road, blocking the Rolls and holding you until the army arrived—it was perfectly obvious that the helicopters had no intention of leaving until you turned up. Once captured, God knows how many of them—especially those who had already served prison terms—would have jumped at the chance of turning state's evidence and incriminating you. It's quite true, you know—there *is* no honor among thieves." If Lord Worth had any objections to being categorized as a thief, it didn't register in his face. "But after the standard bit of soul-searching we decided against it."

"Why, in God's name?"

"So you admit it." Mitchell sighed. "Why couldn't you do that at the beginning and save me all this trouble?"

"Why?" Lord Worth repeated his question.

It was Roomer who answered. "Partly because even though you're a confessed lawbreaker, we still have a regard for you. But mainly because we didn't want to see your daughters confronted with seeing their father behind bars. In hindsight, of course, we're glad we didn't. In comparison with the kidnaping of your daughters, your own capers outside the law fade into a peccadillo."

Mitchell started the motor again and said: "It is understood that there will be no more peccadilloes. It is also understood that there will be no more talk about our taking the law into our own hands."

Lord Worth lay back in his study armchair. His second brandy tasted just as good as his first—it seemed to be his day for brandies. He hadn't spoken a word for the rest of the trip—which, fortunately, had been mercifully short, for Lord Worth had felt urgently in need of restoratives. Not for the first time, he found himself silently blessing his kidnaped daughters.

He cleared his throat and said: "I assume you are still willing to come out to the rig with me?"

Mitchell contemplated his glass. "We never expressed our intentions one way or another about that. But I suppose someone has to look after you and your daughters."

Lord Worth frowned. There had, he felt, been more than a subtle change in their relationship. Perhaps the establishment of an employer-employee status would help redress the balance. He said: "I feel it's time we put your co-operation on a businesslike footing. I propose to retain you in your professional capacities as investigators—in other words, become your client. I shall not quibble at your demanded fees." He had no sooner finished than he realized that he had made a mistake.

Roomer's voice was coldly unenthusiastic. "Money doesn't buy everything, Lord Worth.

Particularly, it doesn't buy us. We have no intention of being shackled, of having our freedom of action curtailed. And as far as the fees and your sky's-the-limit implication are concerned, the hell with it. How often do we have to tell you we don't trade money for your daughters' lives?"

Lord Worth didn't even bother frowning. The change in relationship, he reflected sadly, had been even greater than he had realized. "As you will. One assumes that you will be suitably disguised?"

Mitchell said: "Why?"

Lord Worth was impatient. "You said you saw some ex-convicts boarding the helicopter. People you recognized. They'll surely recognize you?"

"We never saw 'em before in our lives."

Lord Worth was properly shocked. "But you told me——"

"You told us big black lies. What's a little white lie? We'll go aboard as—say—your technological advisers. Geologists, seismologists— it's all the same to us, we know nothing about geology or seismology. All we need are business suits, horn-rimmed glasses—for the studious look—and briefcases." He paused. "And we'll also need a doctor, with full medical kit and a large supply of bandages."

"A doctor?"

"For extracting bullets, sewing up gunshot wounds. Or are you naïve enough to believe that no shot will be fired in anger aboard the *Sea-witch?*"

"I abhor violence."

"Sure. That's why you sent twenty heavily armed thugs out to the *Seawitch* during the night? Fine, so you abhor violence. Others welcome it. Can you find us a doctor?"

"Dozens of them. The average doctor hereabouts rates his scanning of X-rays a very poor second to the scanning of his bank balances. I know the man. Greenshaw. After seven years in Vietnam, he should fill your bill."

Roomer said: "And ask him to bring along two spare white hospital coats."

"Why?" Mitchell said.

"Want to look scientific, don't you?"

Lord Worth picked up the phone, made the arrangements, replaced the instrument and said: "You must excuse me. I have some private calls to make from the radio room." Lord Worth's sole reason for returning to his house was to contact his inside man, Corral, and have him, without incriminating himself, inform Benson, who had hosted the Lake Tahoe meeting, that the government intended to blast out of the water any foreign naval ships that approached the *Seawitch.* An exaggeration but, Lord Worth thought, a pardonable one. Despite the secretary's promise, Lord Worth placed more faith in his direct approach.

Mitchell said: "Which one of us do you want to go with you?"

"What do you mean? 'Private,' I said." His face darkened in anger. "Am I to be ordered around in my own house, supervised as if I'm an irresponsible child?"

"You behaved responsibly last night? Look, Lord Worth, if you don't want either of us around, then it's obvious you want to say something that you don't want us to hear." Mitchell gave him a speculative look. "I don't like that. You're either up to something we wouldn't like, something shady maybe, or it's a vote of no confidence in us."

"It's a personal and highly important business call. I don't see why you should be privy to my business affairs."

Roomer said: "I agree. But it so happens that we don't think it is a business call, that business would be the last thing in your mind right now." Both Mitchell and Roomer stood up. "Give our regards to the girls—if you ever find them."

"Blackmail! Damned blackmail!" Lord Worth rapidly weighed the importance of his call to Corral compared to the importance of having Mitchell and Roomer around. It took all of two seconds to make up his mind, and Corral was clear out of sight at the wire. He was sure that the two men were bluffing, but there was no way he could call their bluff, for that was the one sure way of provoking a genuine walkout.

Lord Worth put on his stony face. "I suppose I have no option other than to accede to your threats. I suggest you go and pack your bags and I'll pick you up in the Rolls."

Mitchell said: "Packing will take some time. I think it would be more polite if we wait here until you're ready."

Lord Worth mentally gnashed his teeth. "You think I'd head for a telephone the moment your backs are turned?"

Mitchell smiled. "Funny the same thought should occur to the three of us at the same instant, isn't it?"

Chapter 7

COMMANDER Larsen and Scoffield observed the approach of the North Hudson helicopter with surprise but without undue concern. Lord Worth customarily gave advance warning of his arrival but could occasionally be forgetful on this point. In any event it was his helicopter and just about his expected time of arrival. They sauntered across the platform and arrived at the northeast helipad just as the helicopter touched down.

Surprisingly, no one emerged immediately from the machine. Larsen and Scoffield looked at each other in some perplexity, a perplexity that was considerably deepened when the disembarkation door slid back and Durand appeared in the doorway with a machine pistol cradled in his hands. Just behind him stood a similarly equipped henchman. From their shadowed position it was impossible for them to be observed by any of the rig duty crew.

Durand said: "Larsen and Scoffield? If you are carrying weapons, please don't be so foolish as to try to use them." The boarding steps swung down. "Come and join us."

The two men had no option. Once aboard, without taking his eyes off them, Durand said: "Kowenski, Rindler—see if they're armed."

Both Larsen and Scoffield carried automatics but seemed quite indifferent to being deprived of them: their attention was directed exclusively to the presence of Lord Worth's daughters.

Marina smiled, albeit a trifle wanly. "We could have met under happier circumstances, Commander."

Larsen nodded. "Your kidnapers. This can carry a death sentence." He looked at Campbell. "Why did you fly those criminals out here?"

"Because I get very cowardly when I have a pistol barrel stuck in the back of my neck all the way from takeoff to touchdown." Campbell spoke with a certain justifiable bitterness.

Larsen looked at Melinda. "Have you been mistreated in any way?"

"No."

"And they won't be," Durand said. "Unless, of course, you refuse to do as we tell you."

"What does that mean?"

"You close down the Christmas tree." This meant closing off all the oil supplies from the ocean floor.

"I'll be damned if I do." Larsen's dark piratical face was suffused with fury. Here, Durand realized, was a man who, even without arms, could be highly dangerous. He glanced briefly at Rindler, who struck Larsen on the back of the neck with his machine pistol, a blow calculated to daze but not knock out. When Larsen's head had cleared he found that he had handcuffs and shackles around wrists and ankles. His attention then focused on a pair of gleaming stainless-steel medical cutters of the type favored by the surgical fraternity for snipping through ribs. The handles were in Durand's firm grip: the unpleasant operating end was closed lightly round the little finger of Melinda's right hand.

Durand said: "Lord Worth isn't going to like you too much for this, Larsen."

Larsen, apparently, was of the same opinion. "All right, take those damned pliers away and get these bracelets off. I'll close down your damned Christmas tree."

"And I'll come with you just to see that you really do turn it off. Not that I would recognize one if I saw it, but I do know that there are such things as flow gauges. I'll be carrying a walkie-talkie with me. Rindler here has another. I'll keep in constant contact with him. If anything should happen to me—" Durand looked consideringly at the medical cutters, then handed them to Heffer, the fifth man in his team. He told Campbell to put his arms behind his seat back and handcuffed his wrists.

"Don't miss much, do you?" Larsen's voice was sour.

"You know how it is. So many villains around these days. Come on."

The two men walked across the platform in the direction of the drilling rig. After only a few paces Durand stopped and looked around him admiringly.

"Well, well, now. Dual-purpose antiaircraft guns. Piles of depth charges. You'd almost think you're prepared to withstand a siege. Dear me, dear me. Federal offense you know. Lord Worth, even with the millions he can pay for lawyers, can get at least ten years in the pen for this."

"What're you talking about?"

"Hardly standard equipment aboard an oil rig. I'll bet it wasn't here twenty-four hours ago. I'll bet it was inside the Mississippi naval arsenal that was broken into last night. The Government takes a dim view of people who steal military equipment. And, of course, you got to have specialists aboard who're skilled at handling stuff like that, and that's hardly part of the basic training of oil-rig crews. I wonder if those crews are also carrying special equipment—like, for instance, what was stolen from a Florida arsenal last night. I mean, two unrelated arsenal break-ins in the same night is too much coincidence. Twenty years in prison, with no chance of parole for you too, for aiding and abetting. And people call *us* criminals."

Larsen had a few choice observations to make in return, none of which would have received the approval of even the most tolerant board of censors.

The Christmas tree was duly neutralized. The pressure gauges registered zero. Durand turned his attention to the *Roamer*, carrying out its short and wearisome patrol between the rig and the huge floating oil tank. "What's our friend up to?"

"Even a landlubber like you ought to be able to guess. He's patrolling the pipeline."

"What the hell for? You could replace a cut line in a day. What would that get anybody? It's crazy."

"You have to use crazy methods to deal with crazy people. From all accounts, Lord Worth's enemies should be locked up for their own good. For everybody's good."

"Worth's band of cutthroats aboard this rig— who's their leader?"

"Giuseppe Palermo."

"That mobster! So the noble Lord, along with

his grand larceny, is an associate of convicted felons."

"You know him, then?"

"Yeah." Durand saw no point in elaborating upon the fact that he and Palermo had spent two prison terms together. "I want to talk to him."

The talk was brief and one-sided. Durand said: "We've got Lord Worth's daughters prisoner. We're going to bring them toward the living quarters here, but we don't want you taking our two aces away from us. You'll stay inside in your quarters. If you don't you're gonna hear a lot of screaming and see pieces of fingers or ears dropped through your windows. I hope you believe me."

Palermo believed him. Palermo had a reputation for ruthlessness that matched Durand's, but it couldn't begin to match Durand's unholy joy in sadism. Durand was perfectly capable of not only doing what he threatened but of deriving immense satisfaction in so doing.

Palermo returned to his Oriental quarters. Durand called up Rindler on the walkie-talkie and told them all to come across, including Campbell, the pilot. Campbell was tough and resourceful and it was just possible that, by standing up, he could slip his manacled arms over the back of his seat, step through them and take off. Whether he would have enough fuel for the return flight would be a problem for him, even though he would almost certainly head not for Florida but for the nearest spot on the mainland, which would be due south of New Orleans.

As the prisoners and guards disembarked from the helicopter Durand said: "Accommodations?"

"Plenty. There are spare rooms in the oriental quarters. There's Lord Worth's private suite."

"Lockups?"

"What do you mean? This isn't a prison."

"Storerooms? Ones that can be locked from the outside?"

"Yes."

Durand looked at Larsen consideringly. "You're being very co-operative, Larsen. Your reputation says otherwise."

"Two minutes' walk around and you could confirm all I'm saying for yourself."

"You'd like to kill me, wouldn't you, Larsen?"

"When the time is ripe, yes. But it's not yet ripe."

"Even so." Durand produced a pistol. "Stay about ten feet away. You might be tempted to grab me and try to make the men let the girls go. A tempting thought, no?"

Larsen looked at him yearningly and said nothing.

The girls, the pilots and their four escorts arrived. Durand said: "Well, now, we gotta find some suitable overnight accommodation for you." He led the way to the first of several storehouses and opened the door to reveal a room packed roof-high with canned goods. He shoved Campbell inside, locked the door and pocketed the key. The next storehouse contained coils of rope, a powerful smell of crude oil and an active, scuttling population of those indestructible creatures, cockroaches. Durand said to the two girls: "Inside."

The girls took one shuddering look, then turned away. Marina said: "We will not go inside that disgusting place."

Kowenski said in a gently chiding voice which accorded ill with the Colt he held in his hand: "Do you know what this is?" Rindler had a similar weapon trained on Melinda.

Both girls glanced briefly at each other and then, in what was obviously a prepared and rehearsed movement, walked toward the men with the guns, seized the barrels with their right hands and hooked their right thumbs behind their trigger forefingers, pulling the guns hard against themselves.

"Jesus Christ!" Durand was badly shaken; he had run up against many situations in his life, but this one lay far beyond his most remote conception. "You trying to commit suicide?"

Melinda said: "Precisely." Her eyes never left Rindler's. "You're lower than those horrible cockroaches in there. You are vermin who are trying to destroy our father. With us dead, you won't have a single card left to play."

"You're crazy! Simple plain crazy!"

"Maybe," Marina said. "But for crazy people our logic is pretty good. With nothing to tie his hands you can imagine how our father will react—especially since he and everyone else will believe that you murdered us. He won't have to go to the law, of course—you simply have no idea what power a few billion dollars can bring to bear. He'll destroy you and all your people to the last man." She looked at Kowenski with contempt. "Why don't you press the trigger? No? Then let go your gun." Kowenski released his gun and Rindler did the same, and the girls dropped them to the deck.

Melinda said: "My sister and I are taking a walk. We will return when you have quarters prepared fitting for Lord Worth's daughters."

Durand's face had definitely lost color and his voice was hoarse and not quite steady as he tried to regain a measure of authority. "So take your walk. Heffer, go with them. Any trouble, shoot them in the legs."

Marina stooped, picked up Kowenski's Colt, walked up to Heffer and rammed the muzzle into his left eye. Heffer recoiled, howling in agony. Marina said: "Fair deal. You shoot me through the leg—now, I mean—and I'll blow your brains out."

"God's sake!" Durand's voice was almost imploring. He was one step removed from wringing his hands. "Somebody's got to go with you. If you're out there on your own and in no danger, Palermo's men will cut us to pieces."

"What a perfectly splendid idea." Marina lowered the pistol and looked in distaste at Heffer, a rodent-faced creature of indeterminate age and nationality. "We see your point. But this—this animal is not to approach within ten yards of us at any time. That is understood?"

"Yes, yes, of course." If they asked him for the moon, Durand would have somehow levitated himself and got it for them. Having overwhelmingly displayed what it was to have seventeen generations of highland aristocratic ancestry behind them, the two girls walked away toward one of the triangular perimeters. It was fully twenty yards before they both began, at the same instant, to tremble violently. Once started, they could not control the trembling and they prayed that the following Heffer could not notice it.

Marina whispered shakily: "Would you do that again?"

"Never, never, never. I'd die."

"I think we came pretty close to it. Do you think that Michael and John would be shaking like us after an experience like that?"

"No. If there's any truth in what Daddy hints, they'd already be planning what to do next. And Durand and his obnoxious friends wouldn't be shaking either. Dead men don't shake very much."

Marina's trembling turned into a genuine

shiver. "I only wish to God they were here right now."

They stopped ten feet short of the platform perimeter. Neither girl had a head for heights. They turned and looked northeastward as the distant and muted roar of an aircraft engine came to their ears.

Durand and Larsen heard it at the same time. They could see nothing because dusk had already fallen, but neither man had any doubt as to the identity of the approaching helicopter and its occupants. With some satisfaction Durand said: "Company. This has to be Lord Worth. Where will they land?"

"The southeast helipad."

Durand glanced across the platform to where the two girls were standing with Heffer, gun carried loosely in his right hand, less than the regulation ten yards away. Satisfied, Durand picked up his machine pistol and said: "Let's go and welcome his lordship aboard. Aaron, come with us."

Larsen said: "You'd better hope Lord Worth proves more tractable than his daughters."

"What do you mean?"

Larsen smiled in sardonic satisfaction. "You caught a couple of tigresses by the tails, didn't you?"

Durand scowled and walked away, followed by Larsen and Aaron, the latter armed similarly to Durand. They reached the southeast helipad just as the North Hudson helicopter touched down. Lord Worth himself was the first out. He stood at the foot of the steps and stared in disbelief at the armed men. He said to Larsen: "What in God's name goes on here?"

Durand said: "Welcome aboard the *Seawitch*, Lord Worth. You can regard me as your host and yourself as a guest—an honored guest, of course. There has been a slight change of ownership."

"I'm afraid that this man here—his name is Durand and I assume that he is one of Cronkite's lieutenants—"

"Cronkite!" Durand was jarred. "What do you know about Cronkite?"

"I can hardly congratulate him on his choice of lieutenants." When Lord Worth poured on his icy contempt he used a king-sized trowel. "Do you think we are such fools as not to know who your employer is? Not that Cronkite has long to live. Nor you, either, for that matter." Durand stirred uneasily—Lord Worth sounded far too much like his daughters for his peace of mind. Lord Worth directed his attention to Larsen. "One assumes that this ruffian arrived with accomplices. How many?"

"Four."

"Four! But with Palermo and his men you have over twenty! How is it possible—"

Durand was back on balance. When he spoke

it was with a slight, if logical, smugness. "We have something that Larsen hasn't. We have your daughters."

What was apparently pure shock rendered Lord Worth temporarily speechless; then in a hoarse voice he said: "Great God almighty! My daughters!" Lord Worth could have had his Oscar just for the asking. "You—*you* are the kidnaper?"

"Fortunes of war, sir." It said much for Lord Worth's aristocratic magnetism that even the most villainous eventually addressed him in respectful tones. "Now, if we could see the rest of the passengers."

Mitchell and Roomer descended. In tan alpaca suits and horn-rimmed glasses they were innocuousness personified. Lord Worth said: "Mitchell and Roomer. Scientists—geologists and seismologists." He turned to Mitchell and Roomer and said dully: "They're holding my daughters captive aboard the *Seawitch*."

"Good God!" Mitchell was properly shocked. "But surely this is the last place—"

"Of course. The unexpected, keeping a couple of steps ahead of the opposition. What'd you come here for?"

"To find new sources of oil. We have a perfectly equipped laboratory here—"

"You could have saved your time. Can we search your bag and your friend's?"

"Have I any choice?"

"No."

"Go ahead."

"Aaron."

Aaron carried out a quick examination of Mitchell's bag. "Clothes. Some scientific books and scientific instruments. Is all."

Dr. Greenshaw clambered down the ladder, reached up and relieved the pilot of various bags and boxes. Durand looked at the door and said: "Who the hell is he?"

"Dr. Greenshaw," Lord Worth said. "A highly respected doctor and surgeon. We did expect a certain amount of violence aboard the *Seawitch*. We came prepared. We do have a dispensary and small sick bay here."

"Another wasted trip. We hold all the cards, and violence is the last thing we expect. We'll examine your equipment too, Doctor."

"If you wish. As a doctor, I deal in life and not in death. I have no concealed weapons. The medical code forbids it." Greenshaw sighed. "Please search but do not destroy."

Durand pulled out his walkie-talkie. "Send one of Palermo's men across here with an electric truck—there's quite a bit of equipment to pick up." He replaced his walkie-talkie and looked at Mitchell. "Your hands are shaking. Why?"

"I'm a man of peace," Mitchell said. He crossed his hands behind his back to conceal the tremor.

Roomer, the only man to recognize the signals, licked his lips and looked at Mitchell in exaggerated nervous apprehension. Durand said: "Another hero. I hate cowards."

Mitchell brought his hands in front of him. The tremor was still there. Durand stepped forward, his right hand swinging back as if to strike Mitchell open-handed, then let his hand fall in disgust, which was, unwittingly, the wisest thing he could have done. Durand's mind was incapable of picking up any psychic signals: had it been so attuned, he could not have failed to hear the black wings of the bird of death flapping above his head.

The only person who derived any satisfaction, carefully concealed, from this vignette, was Larsen. Although he had talked to Mitchell on the telephone he had never met him—but he had heard a great deal about him from Lord Worth, more than enough to make him realize that Mitchell would have reduced Durand to mincemeat sooner than back down before him. Mitchell had taken only seconds to establish the role he wished to establish—that of the cowardly nonentity who could be safely and contemptuously ignored. Larsen, who was no mean hand at taking care of people himself, felt strangely comforted.

Lord Worth said: "May I see my daughters?"

Durand considered, then nodded. "Search him, Aaron."

Aaron, carefully avoiding Lord Worth's basilisk glare of icy outrage, duly searched. "He's clean, Mr. Durand."

"Across there." Durand pointed through the gathering gloom. "By the side of the platform."

Lord Worth walked off without a word. The others made their way toward the accommodation quarters. As Lord Worth approached his daughters, Heffer barred his way.

"Where do you think you're going, mister?"

"Lord Worth to you, peasant."

Heffer pulled out his walkie-talkie. "Mr. Durand? There's a guy here——"

Durand's voice crackled over the receiver. "That's Lord Worth. He's been searched and he's got my permission to speak to his daughters."

Lord Worth plucked the walkie-talkie from Heffer. "And would you please instruct this individual to remain outside listening range?"

"You heard, Heffer." The walkie-talkie went dead.

The reunion between father and daughters was a tearful and impassioned one, at least on the daughters' side. Lord Worth was all that a doting parent reunited with his kidnaped children should have been, but his effusiveness was kept well under control. Marina was the first to notice this.

"Aren't you *glad* to see us again, Daddy?"

Lord Worth hugged them both and said simply: "You two are my whole life. If you don't know that by this time, you will never know it."

"You've never said that before." Even in the deepening dusk it was possible to see the sheen of tears in Melinda's eyes.

"I did not think it necessary. I thought you always knew. Perhaps I'm a remiss parent, perhaps still too much the reserved highlander. But all my billions aren't worth a lock of your black hair, Marina, or a lock of your red hair, Melinda."

"Titian, Daddy, titian. How often must I tell you?" Melinda was openly crying now.

It was Marina, always the more shrewd and perceptive of the two, who put her finger on it. "You aren't surprised to see us, Daddy, are you? You *knew* we were here."

"Of course I knew."

"How?"

"My agents," Lord Worth said loftily, "lie thick upon the ground."

"And what is going to happen now?"

Lord Worth was frank. "I'm damned if I know."

"We saw three other men come off the helicopter. Didn't recognize them—getting too dark."

"One was a Dr. Greenshaw. Excellent surgeon."

Melinda said: "What do you want a surgeon for?"

"Don't be silly. What does anyone want a surgeon for? You think we're going to hand over the *Seawitch* on a platter?"

"And the other two?"

"You don't know them. You've never heard of them. And if you do meet them you will give no indication that you recognize them or have ever seen them before."

Marina said: "Michael and John."

"Yes. Remember—you've never seen them before."

"We'll remember," the girls said almost in chorus. Their faces were transformed. Marina said: "But they'll be in great danger. Why are they here?"

"Something to do, I understand, with their stated intent of taking you back home."

"How are they going to do that?"

Again Lord Worth was frank. "I don't know. If they know, they wouldn't tell me. They've become bossy, very bossy. Watch me like a hawk: Won't even let me near my own blasted phone." The girls refrained from smiling, principally because Lord Worth didn't seem particularly perturbed. "Mitchell, especially, seems in a very tetchy mood." Lord Worth spoke with some relish. "Near as a whisker killed Durand inside the first minute. Would have, too, if you weren't being held hostage. Well, let's go to my suite. I've been to Washington and back. Long tiring day. I need refreshment."

Durand went into the radio room, told the regular operator that his services would not be required until further notice and that he was to return to his quarters and remain there. The operator left. Durand, himself an expert radio operator, raised the *Georgia* within a minute and was speaking to Cronkite thirty seconds later.

"Everything under control on the *Seawitch*. We have the two girls here and Lord Worth himself."

"Excellent." Cronkite was pleased. Everything was going his way, but, then, he had expected nothing else. "Lord Worth bring anyone with him?"

"The pilot and three other people. A doctor—surgeon, he says, and he seems on the level. Worth seems to have expected some blood to be spilled. I'll check his credentials in Florida in a few minutes. Also, two technicians—seismologists, or something like them. Genuine and harmless—the sight of a machine pistol gives them St. Vitus's Dance. They're unarmed."

"So no worries?"

"Well, three. Worth has a squad of about twenty men aboard. They look like trained killers and I'm pretty sure they're all ex-military. They have to be because of my second worry—Worth has eight dual-purpose antiaircraft guns bolted to the platform."

"The hell he has!"

"Yeah—also piles of mines on the sides of the

platform. Now we know who heisted the Mississippi naval arsenal last night. And the third problem is that we're far too thin on the ground. There's only me and four others to watch everybody. Some of us have to sleep sometimes. I need reinforcements and I need 'em fast."

"You'll have over twenty arriving at dawn tomorrow morning. The relief rig crew are due in then. A man named Gregson—you'll recognize him by the biggest red beard you ever saw—will be in charge."

"I can't wait that long. I need reinforcements now. You have your chopper on the *Georgia*."

"What do you think I carry on the *Georgia,* an army of reinforcements?" Cronkite paused, then went on reluctantly: "I can spare eight men, no more."

"They have radar aboard."

"So they have radar. What difference does it make? You're in command."

"Yeah, Mr. Cronkite. But your own golden rule—never take a chance."

"When you hear our helicopter has taken off, neutralize it."

"Destroy the radar cabin?"

"No. We're going to want to use it when we've completely taken over. The scanner will be on top of the drilling derrick. Right?"

"Right."

"It's a simple mechanical job to stop it from turning. All you need is someone with a wrench and a head for heights. Now tell me exactly where Worth's men are quartered. Gregson will need this information."

Durand told him what he wanted to know and hung up.

The dispensary-sick bay and the laboratory were next to each other. Mitchell and Roomer were helping Dr. Greenshaw unpack his very considerable amount of medical equipment. They were, understandably, not unguarded, but Aaron and his Schmeisser were on watch on the two outside doors, and Aaron was hardly in an alert or trigger-ready state of mind. In fact, he regarded his vigil as being close to pointless. He had been present when the three men disembarked from the helicopter and had formed the same opinion of them as Durand.

In the sick bay Dr. Greenshaw up-ended and removed the false bottom of one of his medical supply boxes. With a gingerly and patently nervous apprehension, he took out two belt holsters, two Smith & Wesson .38s, two silencers and two spare magazines. Wordlessly, Mitchell and Roomer buckled on the weaponry. Dr. Greenshaw, a man, as they were discovering, of a genuinely devout turn of mind, said: "I only hope no one discovers you wearing those pistols."

Roomer said: "We appreciate your concern, Doctor. But don't worry about us."

"I wasn't worrying about you." Dr. Greenshaw assumed his most somber expression. "A good Christian can also pray for the souls of the ungodly."

A long distance away the meeting of ten was again assembled at Lake Tahoe. At the former meeting the atmosphere had been hopeful, forceful and determined, the participants confident that things would go their way, spuriously motivated by their expressed intent to avert a third world war. On this evening the spirit—if that was the word—of the meeting had changed about by 180 degrees. They were depressed, vacillating, uncertain and wholly lacking in confidence, especially in view of the fact that their allegedly humanitarian attempts to prevent the outbreak of war seemed to be having precisely the opposite effect.

Again, as it was his holiday home, Benson was hosting the meeting. But this time Benson was also undoubtedly the man in charge. Opening the discussion, he said: "Gentlemen, we are in trouble. Not just simple, plain trouble, but enormous trouble that could bring us all down. It stems from two facts—we underestimated Lord Worth's extraordinary power and we overestimated Cronkite's ability to handle the situation with a suitable degree of discretion and tact. I admit I was responsible for introducing Cronkite to you, but on the other hand, you were unanimous in your belief that Cronkite was the only man to handle the job. And we were not aware that Cronkite's detestation of Lord Worth ran to the extent of a virulent and irresponsible hatred.

"I have friends in the Pentagon, not important ones but ones that matter. The Pentagon, normally, like any other department of government, leaks secrets like a broken sieve. This time I had to pay twenty thousand dollars to a stenographer and the same to a cipher clerk which, for a pair of comparatively lowly paid government employees, represents a pretty fair return for a few hours' work.

"First, everything is known about our previous meeting here, every word and sentiment that was expressed and the identities of all of us." Benson paused and looked round the room, partly to allow time for the damning enormity of this information to sink in, partly to make it clear that he expected to be recompensed for his very considerable outlay.

Mr. A, one of the vastly powerful Arabian Gulf potentates, said: "I thought our security was one hundred per cent. How could anyone have known of our presence?"

"No external agency was involved. I have good friends in California intelligence. Their interest in us is zero. Nor was the FBI involved. For that to have happened we'd have had to commit some crime and then cross state lines.

Neither of those have we done. And before we met last time I had an electronics expert in to check not only this room but the entire house for bugs. There were none."

Mr. A said: "Perhaps *he* planted a bug?"

"Impossible. Apart from the fact that he's an old friend of immaculate reputation, I was with him all the time, a fact that did not prevent me from calling in a second expert."

Patinos, the Venezuelan, said: "We give you full marks for security. That leaves only one possibility. One of us here is a traitor."

"Yes."

"Who?"

"I have no idea. We shall probably never know."

Mr. A stroked his beard. "Mr. Corral here lives very close to Lord Worth, no?"

Corral said: "Thank you very much."

Benson said: "Intelligent men don't make so obvious a link."

"As you said at our previous meeting, I'm the only person who had no declared interest in being here." Borosoff seemed quietly relaxed. "I could be your man."

"It's a point, but one which I don't accept. Whether you are here to stir up trouble between the United States and Russia may or may not be the case. Again it comes down to the factor of intelligence." Benson was being disarmingly frank. "You could be, and probably are, a Soviet agent.

But top agents are never caught in the role of *agent provocateur*. I am not complimenting you on your unquestioned intelligence. I prefer to rely on simple common sense." Benson, who appeared to have developed a new maturity and authority, looked around the company. "Every word spoken here will doubtless be relayed to either Lord Worth or the State Department. It no longer matters. We are here to set right any wrongs for which we may have been—however unwittingly, I may say—responsible.

"We know that a Russian missile naval craft and a Russian-built Cuban submarine are closing in on the *Seawitch*. We also know that a Venezuelan destroyer is doing the same. What you don't know is that countermeasures are being taken. My information—and the source is impeccable—is that Lord Worth was today closeted with Benton, the Secretary of State, in Washington. My further information is that Benton was only partially convinced by Lord Worth's suspicions. He was, unfortunately, wholly convinced when the news came through of Cronkite's irresponsible folly in kidnaping Lord Worth's two daughters. As a result, a United States cruiser and destroyer, both armed with the most sophisticated weaponry, have moved out into the Gulf of Mexico. An American nuclear submarine is already patrolling those waters. Another American vessel is already shadowing your destroyer, Mr. Patinos: your destroyer, with its vastly inferior detecting equipment, is wholly unaware of this. Additionally, at a Louisiana air base, a squadron of supersonic fighter-bombers is on instant alert.

"The Americans are no longer in any mood to play around. My information is that they are prepared for a showdown and are prepared for the eyeball-to-eyeball confrontation which John Kennedy had with Khrushchev over Cuba. The Russians, clearly, would never risk a local nuclear confrontation where the home-territory advantages are so overwhelmingly American. Neither side would dream of mounting a pre-emptive strike over the issue of a few pennies on a barrel of oil. But if the hot line between Washington and Moscow begins to burn, national prestige will make it difficult for either side to back down until they arrive at a face-saving formula, which could take quite some time and would, much worse, generate overwhelming worldwide publicity. This would inevitably involve us. So I would advise you, Mr. Borosoff and Mr. Patinos, to call off your dogs of war before that hot line starts burning. That way, and only in that way, can we survive with our good names left unbesmirched. I blame neither of you gentlemen. You may have given the nod to Cronkite, but you did not reckon on the possibility that Cronkite would carry matters to such ridiculous lengths. Please, please believe me that the Americans will not hesitate to blast your ships out of the water."

Oil ministers do not become oil ministers because they are mentally retarded. Patinos smiled a smile of wry resignation. "I do not relish the thought of personal ruin. Nor do I relish the thought of becoming a scapegoat for my government." He looked across at Borosoff. "We call off the dogs of war?"

Borosoff nodded. "Back to their kennels and no alas. I wish to return to my Russia and this will give me great face, for they will not have to lose face in the world."

Mr. A leaned back in his chair. His relief was manifest. "Well, that would seem to cover that."

"It covers most of it," Benson said. "But not all. Another very unpleasant and potentially terrifying crime occurred this afternoon. I heard of it only an hour ago and it will be the hottest topic in the nation tonight. I only hope to God that, although we were in no way responsible for it, we won't be implicated in it. A place called Netley Rowan Arsenal was broken into this afternoon. It's supposed to be just another arms depot insofar as the public is concerned— and so, mainly, it is. But it's also a TNW arsenal. TNW means 'tactical nuclear weapons.' Two of them were stolen in the break-in and appear to have vanished without trace."

"God above!" The expression and tone of the

man from Honduras accurately reflected the shocked feelings of all around the table. "Cronkite?"

"I'd bet on it. No proof, naturally, but who the hell else?"

Henderson said: "No disrespect to Mr. Borosoff here, but couldn't the Russians, say, have been seeking a prototype?"

Benson looked as weary as his voice sounded. "The Russians already have God knows how many of those things. It's public knowledge that they have thousands of them deployed along the border between the Warsaw pact and NATO countries—many of them, it is suspected, more sophisticated than ours. The Russians need our TNWs the way they need bows and arrows." Borosoff, despite the anxiety he shared with the others, permitted himself the ghost of a smile of complacency. "Cronkite. The man's running wild."

Mr. A said: "You think he's so totally crazy as to use a nuclear device against the *Seawitch?*"

"I do not profess to understand the workings of an obviously diseased mind," Benson said. "He's capable of anything."

Patinos said: "What's this weapon like?"

"I don't know. I phoned the Pentagon, a very senior official there, but although he's an old friend of mine, he refused to release highly classified information. All I know is that it can be used as a land-based time bomb—I suppose that includes the sea as well—or as an aircraft bomb. It can only be used in a limited number of super-sonic fighter-bombers, which will already, I suppose, be under the heaviest security guard ever, which would strike me as a superfluous precaution as there is no chance that Cronkite, even with his obviously wide range of contacts, could know anyone who could fly one of those planes."

"So what happens?"

"I think we'd better consult an astrologer on that one. All I know is that Cronkite has gone stark raving mad."

Cronkite, aboard the *Georgia*, would have thought the same of them. He had a job to do and he was doing it to the best of his ability. Had he known of the possible withdrawal of the warships that had sailed from Cuba and Vene-zuela, he would not have been unduly concerned. He had had some vague idea that they might have been useful to him in some way, but he had primarily wished to have them as a cover and a smokescreen. Cronkite's vendetta against Lord Worth was a highly personal and extremely vindictive one and he wanted no other than himself to administer the *coup de grace*. Retri-bution exacted through the medium of other hands would not do at all.

Meantime, he was well content. He was con-vinced that the *Seawitch* was in his hands.

Come the dawn it would be doubly in his hands. He knew of their defenses and radar. The *Starlight,* under Easton, was waiting until full darkness before it moved in for the initial attack, and as rain had been falling steadily for some time now and the lowering sky blotted out the quarter-moon, it promised to be as nearly dark as it ever becomes at sea.

A message was brought to him from the radio office. Cronkite glanced at it briefly, picked up the phone to the helipad and reached the pilot in his shelter. "Ready to go, Wilson?"

"Whenever you say, Mr. Cronkite."

"Then, now." Cronkite closed a rheostat switch and a dull glow of light outlined the helipad, just enough to let Wilson make a clean takeoff. The helicopter made a half-circle, switched on its landing light and made a smooth landing on the calm waters less than a hundred yards from the stationary *Georgia.*

Cronkite called the radar room. "You have him on the screen?"

"Yes, sir. He's making an instrument approach on our radar."

"Let me know when he's about three miles out."

Less than a minute later the operator gave him the word. Cronkite turned the rheostat to full and the helipad became brilliantly illuminated.

A minute later a helicopter, landing lights on,

appeared from the north through the driving
rain. Just over another minute later it touched
down as delicately as a moth, an understandable
precaution by the pilot, in view of the cargo he
was carrying. The fueling hoses were connected
immediately. The door opened and three men
descended—the alleged Colonel Farquharson,
Lieutenant Colonel Dewings and Major Breckley, who had been responsible for the Netley
Rowan Arsenal break-in. They helped unload
two large, double-handed and obviously very
heavy suitcases. Cronkite, with suitable admoni-
tions as to delicacy in handling, showed crew
members where to stow the cases in shelter.

Within ten minutes the helicopter was on its
way back to the mainland. Five minutes after
that, the *Georgia*'s own helicopter had returned
and all the helipad lights were switched off.

Chapter 8

IT was due only to cruel ill luck and the extremely jittery state of Durand's nerves that John Roomer and Melinda Worth found themselves the first patients in Dr. Greenshaw's sick bay.

Durand was in a highly apprehensive state of mind, a mood that transferred itself all too easily to his four subordinates. Although he held control of the *Seawitch*, he knew that his hold was a tenuous one: he had not bargained on finding Palermo and his cutthroats on board, and even though he held the master keys to both the occidental and oriental quarters in his pocket— the drilling crew was in the former quarters,

Palermo and his men in the latter—he was acutely aware that there were far too many windows in both quarters and he didn't have the men to cover every possible exit. He had broadcast a message over the external loud-speaker that anyone found on the platform would be shot on sight and had two men on constant patrol round the oriental quarters—he had no fear of the unarmed drilling-rig crew—and another two constantly patrolling the platform. He had no fear of Lord Worth, his seismologists and the girls—as sources of danger he held them in contempt. Besides, they were unarmed. Even so, the two men patrolling the platform had been instructed to do so in such a fashion as to make sure that at least one had an eye on the doors to the suite of Lord Worth, the laboratory and the sick bay, all three of which had intercommunicating doors.

No one inside those three places had heard the warning broadcast—and this, ironically, because Lord Worth was not above indulging in what he regarded as the bare minimum of basic creature comforts. Oil rigs can be uncommonly noisy places, and those quarters he had heavily insulated.

Mitchell had been in his tiny cubicle of the laboratory at the time, reading the complete plan of the layout of the *Seawitch* over and over until he was certain that he could have found his way around the rig blindfolded. This had taken him about twenty minutes. It was in the fifth minute of his studying that the shots had been fired, but again, because of the soundproofing, the sound had not reached him. He had just put the plans away in a drawer when his door opened and Marina entered. She was white-faced and shaking and her face was streaked with tears. He put his arms round her and she grabbed him tightly.

"Why weren't you there?" she sobbed. "Why weren't you there? You could have stopped them. You could have saved them!"

Mitchell took no time out to dwell upon the injustices of life. He said gently: "Stopped what? Saved who?"

"Melinda and John. They've been terribly hurt."

"How?"

"Shot."

"Shot? I didn't hear anything."

"Of course you didn't. This area is all sound-proofed. That's why Melinda and John didn't hear the broadcast warning."

"Broadcast warning? Tell it to me slowly."

So she told him as slowly and coherently as she could. There had been such a warning but it had gone unheard in Lord Worth's suite. The rain had stopped, at least temporarily, and when Mitchell had retired to study the plans, Melinda and Roomer had elected to go for a stroll. They had been wandering around the foot of the drilling rig, where most of the lights had been turned off since Durand had ordered the abandonment of drilling, and it was there that they had been gunned down without warning.

"Terribly hurt, you said. How bad?"

"I'm not sure. Dr. Greenshaw is operating in the sick bay. I'm not a coward, you know that, but there was so much blood that I didn't want to look."

Arrived in the sick bay, Mitchell could hardly blame her. Melinda and Roomer lay in adjacent cots and both were saturated with blood. Melinda already had her left shoulder heavily bandaged. Roomer had bandages swathing his neck and Dr. Greenshaw was working on his chest.

Lord Worth, his face a mask of bitter fury, was sitting in a chair. Durand, his face a mask of nothingness, was standing by the doorway. Mitchell looked speculatively at both, then spoke to Dr. Greenshaw. "What can you tell so far, Doctor?"

"Would you listen to him?" Roomer's voice was a hoarse whisper and his face creased with near-agony. "Never think of asking us how *we* feel."

"In a minute. Doctor?"

"Melinda's left shoulder is bad. I've extracted the bullet but she needs immediate surgery. I'm a surgeon, but I'm not an orthopedic surgeon, and that's what she must have. Roomer hasn't been quite so lucky. He got hit twice. The one through the neck missed his carotid artery by a whisker, but the bullet passed straight through and there's no worry there. The chest wound is serious. Not fatal but very serious. The bullet struck the left lung, no doubt about that, but the internal bleeding isn't that much, so I think it's a nick, no more. The trouble is, I think the bullet is lodged against the spine."

"Can he wiggle his toes?"

Roomer moaned. "My God, what sympathy."

"He can. But the bullet should be removed as soon as possible. I could do it but I have no X-ray equipment here. I'll give them both blood transfusions in a moment."

"Shouldn't they be flown to a hospital as soon as possible?"

"Of course."

Mitchell looked at Durand. "Well?"

"No."

"But it wasn't their fault. They didn't hear the warning."

"Tough. There's no way I'll fly them ashore. Think I want a battalion of U. S. Marines out here in a few hours?"

"If they die it'll be your fault."

"Everybody's got to die sometime." Durand left, slamming the door behind him.

"Dear, dear." Roomer tried to shake his head, then winced at the pain in his neck. "He shouldn't have said that."

Mitchell turned to Lord Worth. "You can be

of great help, sir. Your suite is in direct contact with the radio room; can you hear what is being said in the radio room?"

"That's no problem. Two switches and I can hear both sides of any conversation, either on the telephone, earphones or wall receivers."

"All right—go, and don't stop listening for a second." He looked at the two patients on the cots. "We'll have them airborne for the hospital within a half hour."

"How can that be possible?"

"I don't know." Mitchell sounded vague. "But we'll think of something."

Lord Worth left. Mitchell pulled out a slender pencil flashlight and started to flick it on and off in apparent aimlessness. His complexion had gone pale and the hands that held the pencil light trembled slightly. Marina looked at him first uncomprehendingly, then in dismay, finally in something approaching contempt. Incredulously, she said: "You're frightened."

"Your gun?" Mitchell said to Roomer.

"When they went off for help I managed to drag myself a bit nearer the edge. I unclipped the belt and threw the whole thing over the side."

"Good. We're still in the clear." He seemed to become aware of the tremor in his hands, put away his flash and thrust his hands into his pockets. He said to Melinda: "Who shot you?"

"A pair of very unpleasant characters named

Kowenski and Rindler. We had trouble with them before."

"Kowenski and Rindler," Mitchell repeated. He left the sick bay.

Marina said, half in sadness, half in bitterness: "My idol with the feet of clay."

Roomer said huskily: "Put out the light and then put out the light."

"What did you say?"

"*I* didn't say it. Man named Othello. That's the trouble with you millionaires' daughters. Illiterate. First Mitchell puts out the lights. He's got cat's eyes. He can see in almost total darkness where an ordinary man is blind. Did you know that?"

"No."

"Gives him a tremendous advantage. And then he puts out other lights."

"I know what you mean and I don't believe you. I saw him shaking."

"Ahh . . . you don't deserve him."

She stared at him in disbelief. "What did you say?"

"You heard me." Roomer sounded tired and the doctor was looking at him in disapproval. He went on in a somber voice: "Kowenski and Rindler are dead men. They have just minutes to live. He loves Melinda almost as much as he does you, and I've been his closest friend and partner since we were kids. Mitchell looks after his own." He smiled faintly. "I'm afraid he takes care of things in a sort of final way."

"But he was shaking . . ." Her voice was now lacking in conviction.

"He isn't afraid of anything that lives. As for the shaking—he's a throwback to the old Scandinavian berserkers: he's just trying to hold in his rage. He usually smiles." He smiled. "You're shaking now."

She said nothing.

Roomer said: "There's a cupboard in the vestibule. If there's anything in it, bring it to me."

She looked at him uncertainly, left and returned in a few minutes, carrying a pair of shoes. She held them at arm's length and from the look of horror on her face might have been holding a cobra.

Roomer said: "Mitchell's?"

"Yes."

"Okay. Better return them. He'll be needing them pretty soon."

When she came back, Melinda said to her: "Do you really think you could marry a man who kills people?"

Marina shivered and said nothing. Roomer said sardonically: "Better than marrying a coward, I'd say."

In the generator room, Mitchell found what he wanted right away—a circuit breaker marked "Deck Lights." He pulled the lever and stepped out onto the now darkened platform. He waited a half minute until his eyes adjusted themselves to the darkness, then moved in the direction of the derrick crane where he could hear two men cursing in far from muted voices. He approached on soundless stockinged feet until he was less than two yards away. Still soundlessly, he held his pencil flash on top of the barrel of the Smith & Wesson and slid forward the flash switch.

The two men swung round in remarkably swift unison, hands reaching for their guns.

Mitchell said: "You know what this is, don't you?"

They knew. The deep-bluish sheen of a silencer-equipped .38 is not readily mistakable for a popgun. Their hands stopped reaching for their guns. It was, to say the least, rather unnerving to see an illuminated silenced gun and nothing but blackness beyond it.

"Clasp your hands behind your necks, turn round and start walking."

They walked until they could walk no more, for the good reason that they had reached the end of the platform. Beyond that lay nothing but the 200-foot drop to the Gulf of Mexico.

Mitchell said: "Keep your hands clasped and turn round."

They did so. "You're Kowenski and Rindler?"

There was no reply.

"You're the two who gunned down Melinda and Mr. Roomer?"

Again there was no reply. Vocal cords can become paralyzed when the mind is possessed of the irrevocable certainty that one is but one step, one second, removed from eternity. Mitchell squeezed the trigger twice and was walking away before the dead men had hit the waters of the Gulf. He had taken only four steps when a flashlight beam struck him in the face.

"Well, well, if it isn't smart-ass Mitchell, the scared scientist." Mitchell couldn't see the man— and the gun undoubtedly behind the flashlight— but he had no difficulty in recognizing the voice of Heffer, the one with the sharp nose and ratlike teeth. *"And* carrying a silenced gun. Whatcha up to, Mr. Mitchell?"

Heffer had made the classic blunder of all incompetent would-be assassins. He should have shot Mitchell on sight and then asked the questions. Mitchell flicked on his pencil torch and spun it upward, where it spiraled around like a demented firefly. Heffer would have been less than human not to have had the instinctive re-action of glancing upward as his subconscious mind speculated as to what the hell Mitchell was up to: a speculation of very brief duration in-deed, because Heffer was dead before the flash fell back onto the platform.

Mitchell picked up the flash, still surprisingly working, pocketed it, then dragged Heffer by the heels and rolled him off to join his friends at the bottom of the Gulf. He returned to the sick-bay vestibule, donned his shoes and entered the sick bay itself. Dr. Greenshaw had both his patients on blood transfusion.

Roomer looked at his watch. "Six minutes. What took you so long?"

A plainly unnerved Marina looked at Roomer, half in disbelief, half in stupefaction.

"Well, I'm sorry." Mitchell actually managed to sound apologetic. "I had the misfortune to run into Heffer on the way back."

"You mean he had the misfortune to run into you. And where are our friends?"

"I'm not rightly sure."

"I understand." Roomer sounded sympathetic. "It's hard to estimate the depth of the water out here."

"I could find out. But it hardly seems to matter. Dr. Greenshaw, you have stretchers? Complete with straps and so forth?" Greenshaw nodded. "Get them ready. Let them stay where they are meantime. Can you carry on the blood transfusions in flight?"

"That's no problem. I assume you want me to accompany them?"

"Yes, please. I know it's asking an awful lot, but after you've handed them over to the competent medical authorities, I'd like you to return."

"It will be a pleasure. I am now in my seventieth year and I thought there was nothing fresh left in life for me to experience. I was wrong."

Marina stared at them in disbelief. All three

men seemed calm and relaxed. Melinda appeared to have dropped off into a coma-like stupor, but she was merely, in fact, under heavy sedation. Marina said with conviction: "You're all mad."

Mitchell said: "That's what a lunatic asylum inmate says about the outside world—and he may well be right. However, that's hardly the point at issue. You, Marina, will be accompanying the others on the trip back to Florida. You will be perfectly safe there—your father will see that the most massive security guard ever mounted will be there."

"How splendid. I love being made a fuss over, being the center of attraction. However, mastermind, there's just one small flaw in your reasoning. I'm not going. I'm staying with my father."

"That's exactly the point I'm going to discuss with him now."

"You mean you're going out to kill someone else?"

Mitchell held out his hands, fingers splayed. They could have been carved from marble.

"Later," Roomer said. "He appears to have some other things on his mind at the moment."

Mitchell left. Marina turned furiously on Roomer. "You're just as bad as he is."

"I'm a sick man. You mustn't upset me."

"You and his berserker moods. He's just a killer."

Roomer's face went very still. "You know, I

don't look forward to the prospect of having a mentally retarded person as a sister-in-law."

She was shocked and the shock showed. Her voice was a whisper. "I don't really know you, do I?"

"No. We're the men who walk down the dark side of the streets. Somebody has to look after the people on the dark side. *We* do it. Do you know how much your father offered us to take you home?" Roomer smiled. "I'm afraid I'm not much good in that department at the moment, but Mike will take care of it."

"How much did he offer you?"

"Whatever we wanted in the world. A million dollars to take you home? A hundred million if we'd asked for it? Sure."

"How much did you ask for?" Her face wasn't registering much in the way of expression.

Roomer sighed, "Poor Mike. To think that he regards you as the pot of gold at the foot of the rainbow. Poor me, too. I'm going to have to live with you too, even at second hand. Let's be corny. Your father loves you. We love you. To pile cliché on cliché, there are some things that can't be bought. Pearls beyond price. Don't make yourself an artificial pearl, Marina. And don't ever insult us again that way. But we have to live on something, so we'll send him a bill."

"For what?"

"Ammunition expended."

She crossed to his cotside, knelt and kissed

him. Roomer seemed too weak to resist. Dr. Greenshaw was severe. "Marina, he's not only having a blood transfusion, there's also the factor of blood pressure."

Roomer said: "My blood pressure is registering no complaints."

She kissed him again. "Is that apology enough?" Roomer smiled and said nothing. "'Berserker' you said. Can anyone stop him when he's like that? Can I?"

"No. Someday, yes."

"The one person is you. Yes?"

"Yes."

"You didn't."

"No."

"Why?"

"They carried guns."

"You carry guns."

"Yes. But we're not evil people who carry evil guns to do evil things."

"That's all?"

"No." He looked across at Melinda. "You see?"

"Please."

"If Kowenski and Rindler hadn't been such damned lousy shots, she'd be dead."

"So you let Michael loose?"

"Yes."

"You're going to marry her?"

"Yes."

"Have you asked her?"

"No."

"You don't have to. Sisters talk."

"Mike?"

"I don't know, John. I'm a running coward, running scared."

"Well?"

"He kills."

"I've killed."

"He'll kill again?"

"I don't know."

"John."

He reached out, took a lock of her gleaming black hair, picked out a single thread. "That."

"You mean?"

"Yes."

"I have to see." She kicked off her high-heeled shoes.

"So much to learn. Sit."

She sat on his bed. Dr. Greenshaw rolled his eyes heavenward. She was wearing blue jeans and a white blouse. Roomer reached up and undid the top button of her blouse. She looked at him and said nothing. Roomer said: "You do the rest. Navy or black jumper."

She was back in thirty seconds, wearing a navy polo. She looked inquiringly at Roomer, who nodded. She left the sick bay.

In Lord Worth's living room, he and Mitchell were seated in adjacent armchairs. The wall-speakers were on. When Marina came in, Mitchell waved her to urgent silence.

Over the speakers Durand's unmistakable voice sounded testy. "All I know is that the deck lights went out some minutes ago and then came back on." Marina glanced at Mitchell, who nodded. "All the light you need to land."

"Have you neutralized the radar scanner yet?"

Marina had never heard the voice before, but the tightening of Lord Worth's lip showed that Cronkite's voice was no stranger to him.

"We don't need to now."

"It was your idea. Do it. We'll leave in ten minutes, then about fifteen minutes' flying time."

" 'We'll leave'? That mean you're coming too?"

"No. I've more important things to do." There was a click: Cronkite had ceased to transmit.

Lord Worth said uneasily: "I wonder what that devious devil means by that?"

"We'll just have to find out the hard way." Mitchell looked at Marina. "Where are your shoes?"

She smiled sweetly. "I'm a quick study. Shoes make too much noise out on the platform."

"You're not going out on any platform."

"I am. There are gaps in my education. I want to see how killers operate."

Mitchell said in irritation: "I'm not going to kill anyone. Go get your bag packed. You'll be leaving soon."

"I'm not leaving."

"Why?"

"Because I want to stay with Daddy—and with you. Don't you think that's natural?"

"You're leaving if I have to tie you up."

"You can't tie my tongue up. Wouldn't the law just love to know where the guns stolen from the Mississippi arsenal are?"

Lord Worth looked slightly stunned. "You'd do that to me? Your own father?"

"You'd tie me up and force me aboard that helicopter? Your own daughter?"

"Talk about logic." Mitchell shook his head. "Lord Worth seems to have fathered a nutcase. If you think—"

The wallspeakers crackled again. "Well, don't just hang around. Stop that radar."

"How?" It was Aaron and he sounded grieved. "Do you expect me to climb that damned drilling rig—"

"Don't be stupid. Go to the radar room. There's a red lever switch just above the console. Pull it down."

"That I can do." Aaron sounded relieved. They heard the sound of a door closing. Mitchell kicked off his shoes, turned off the lights in the living room and eased the door open a crack. Aaron, his back already to them, was heading for the radar room. He reached it, opened the door and passed inside. Mitchell moved after him, pulling out his silenced gun and holding it in his left hand. A soft voice behind him said: "I thought you were right-handed."

Mitchell didn't even bother to curse. He said in a resigned whisper: "I am."

Aaron was just pulling the red lever when Mitchell made his soundless entrance. He said: "Don't turn round."

Aaron didn't turn round.

"Clasp your hands behind your neck, then turn and come over here."

Aaron turned. "Mitchell!"

"Don't try anything clever. I've already had to kill three of your friends. A fourth isn't going to give me a sleepless night. Stop right there and turn round again."

Aaron did as he was told. Mitchell withdrew his right hand from his coat pocket. The braided leather sap attached to his wrist by a thong was no more than five inches long, but when it struck Aaron with considerable force and accuracy above and behind the right ear it was apparent that five inches was quite long enough. Mitchell caught him as he fell and eased him to the deck.

"Did you have to do that—" Marina choked and stopped speaking involuntarily as Mitchell's hand clamped itself none too gently over her mouth. She flinched as he shook the sap before her eyes.

"Keep your voice down." The whisper was intentionally savage. He knelt over Aaron, removed and pocketed his gun.

"Did you have to do that?" she said in a low

voice. "You could have tied him up and gagged him."

"When I require advice from amateurs I'll come right to you. I haven't time for games. He'll just have a half-hour peaceful rest, and then all he'll need is an aspirin."

"And now?"

"Durand."

"Why?"

"Fool."

"I'm getting tired of people calling me fool. John just called me that. He also said I was mentally retarded and an artificial pearl."

"No shrewder judge of character than old John," Mitchell said approvingly. "If Aaron doesn't return, Durand will come looking for him. Then he'll get on the radiophone and stop the helicopter flight."

"Well, that's what you want, isn't it?"

"No."

He switched off the light and walked away, Marina following. Mitchell stopped outside the entrance to Lord Worth's sitting room.

"Get inside. You're both an irritation and a liability. I can't function properly with you around. Heroines I can do without."

"I promise you I won't say a word. I promise—"

He caught her by the arm and thrust her forcibly inside. Lord Worth looked up in mild surprise. Mitchell said: "I will hold you personally responsible, Lord Worth, if you let this pesky daughter of yours outside that door again. Also, I'm dimming the deck lights. Anybody moving around the platform will be shot. That's my promise and you'd better believe it. This is no place for children who want to play games." The door closed behind him.

"Well!" Marina sat down and gripped her hands together. "What kind of husband do you think *he* would make?"

"A perfectly splendid one, I should imagine. Look, my dear, one of Mitchell's outstanding assets is a hair-trigger reaction. You blunt it. And you know damn well how he feels about you— your presence just constitutes an additional worry at a time when he can least afford either. A wife doesn't accompany her husband down a coal mine or on a wartime bombing mission. And Mitchell is much more of a loner than such people are."

She attempted something between a glower and a scowl, but her beautiful face really wasn't made for it, so she settled for a rueful smile, rose and replenished his glass of malt whisky.

Mitchell removed the gun and two large keys from the pockets of an unconscious Durand, made his way to the main entrance to the oriental quarters, opened the door and switched on the corridor lights.

"Commander Larsen," he called out. "Palermo."

Doors opened and the two men were with him in a few seconds. Larsen said: "Mitchell! What the hell are you doing here?"

"Just a harmless seismologist taking a stroll."

"But didn't you hear the broadcast warning— anyone on the platform will be shot on sight?"

"That's past. One piece of bad news, two of good. Bad news first. Roomer and Miss Melinda didn't hear the warning—those quarters are sound-insulated. So they took a walk. Both were hurt badly. Melinda has a shattered left shoulder. Roomer was shot through the neck and chest. The doctor thinks the bullet is lodged against his spine. We've got to get them to the hospital and quick. Who's Lord Worth's personal pilot?"

"Chambers," Larsen said.

"Get one of your men to have him refuel his machine. Now the good news. Durand is in the radio room; his number two, guy named Aaron, is in the radar room. Both are unconscious." He looked at Palermo. "When they come to—it'll be some time yet—can you have them looked after with loving care and attention?"

"Our pleasure."

Larsen said: "Durand had three other men."

"They're dead."

"You?"

"Yes."

"We didn't hear any shooting."

Mitchell gave them a brief sight of his silenced .38. Larsen looked thoughtful. "Lord Worth has talked about you: I used to think he was exaggerating."

"The other bit of good news. Cronkite is sending some reinforcements by helicopter—not many, I believe, eight or nine—and they should be taking off about now. A fifteen-minute flight, I gather, so I think Cronkite's boat is somewhere just below the horizon, below our radar sweep."

Palermo brightened. "We blast this chopper out of the sky?"

"My first thought, I must admit. But let's try to play it smart and put him off his guard. Let's let them land, then take them. We'll make their leader report to Cronkite that everything's okay."

"What if he won't? Or tries to warn him?"

"We'll write out his script. If he changes one word I'll shoot him. Silencer. Cronkite won't hear it."

"He might hear the guy scream."

"When a .38 slug enters the base of your skull and travels upward at forty-five degrees, you don't scream very much."

"You mean you'd kill him?" While not exactly incredulous, Larsen was obviously taken aback.

"Yes. Then we'd line up number two. We shouldn't have too much trouble with him."

Larsen said with some feeling: "When Lord Worth talked about you he didn't tell me the half of it."

"Another thing. I want that helicopter. We'll fake a story that the engine failed above the pad and it crash-landed, and will take several hours to repair. It's always handy to have another helicopter around but, more important, I want to deprive Cronkite of the use of his." He looked at Palermo. "I take it that the reception committee can be safely left in your hands?"

"It sure can. Any suggestions?"

"Well, I doubt that I need to lecture an expert like you."

"You know me?"

"I used to be a cop. In any case, the rig is loaded with portable searchlights. They'll head for the administration buildings. I'd stay in hiding, switch off the deck lights and then turn on the searchlights when they're, say, thirty yards away. They'll be blinded and won't be able to see you."

"You can't count on what nutcases like that'll do."

"I'll bet *you* can." Mitchell smiled briefly at him, cop to crook. He said to Larsen: "I have a feeling that Lord Worth would like to confer with his rig boss."

"Yes." They walked away as Palermo was already giving rapid instructions to his men. "Lord Worth know what you're up to?"

"I haven't had time. Anyway, I wouldn't tell Lord Worth how to make a billion out of oil."

"Good point." They stopped briefly by the radio room. Larsen gazed at the crumpled form of Durand, half in appreciation, half in regret. "What a beautiful sight. Wish it had been me, though."

"I'll bet Durand—when he wakes up—doesn't. Plastic surgeons come high."

They made their next brief stop at the sick bay. Larsen looked at a still comatose Melinda and a wide-awake Roomer and his massive fists clenched. Roomer smiled. "I know. But you're too late. How deep's the water here?"

"Nine hundred feet."

"Then you'd need a diving bell to get your hands round the throats of those responsible. And how are things with you, Commander Larsen? You can see how things are with us."

"I've been resting. Mitchell has been more active. Besides the three men at the bottom of the Gulf, he's also deprived me of the pleasure of beating the hell out of Durand. Aaron isn't feeling too well either."

Roomer said apologetically: "He doesn't go in much for diplomacy. So the *Seawitch* is in our hands?"

"For the moment."

"For the moment?"

"Do you expect a man like Cronkite to give up? So he's lost five men and is probably about to lose another eight or nine. What's that for a man with ten million to play around with? And he's got his personal vendetta against Lord Worth. If he has to cripple or even destroy the *Seawitch*, including everybody aboard—well, it isn't going to bother Cronkite's conscience for long." He turned to Dr. Greenshaw. "I think it's time you got busy with the stretchers. Can you spare four of your drilling crew, Commander, to help transfer them to the stretchers and then across to the helicopter? I'm afraid, John, you're going to have some unpleasant company on the trip. Durand and Aaron. Tied up like chickens, of course."

"Well, thank you very much."

"I can—occasionally—be as leery as you. I wouldn't put it past Cronkite to get aboard the *Seawitch*. How, I haven't the faintest idea, but with a highly devious mind a driven man can accomplish most anything. If he succeeded I don't want Durand and Aaron blowing the whistle on me. I want to stay an inconspicuous and harmless seismologist."

Larsen gave a few orders on the phone, then he and Mitchell went through to Lord Worth's room. Lord Worth was on the phone, listening and scowling. Marina looked at Mitchell with an expression as forbidding as her father's.

"I suppose you've been littering the platform with a few more dead men?"

"You do me a grave injustice. There's no one

left to kill." She gave what might have been a tiny shudder and looked away.

Larsen said: "The ship is in our hands, Miss Marina. We're expecting a little more trouble in about ten minutes, but we can take care of that."

Lord Worth replaced his receiver. "What's that?"

"Cronkite is sending some reinforcements by helicopter. Not many—eight or nine. They won't have a chance. He's under the impression that Durand is still in charge here."

"I take it he's not."

"He's unconscious and tied up. So is Aaron."

A yearning look came over Lord Worth's face. "Is Cronkite coming with them?"

"No."

"How very unfortunate. And I've just had some more bad news. The *Torbello* has broken down."

"Sabotage?"

"No. The main fuel-supply line to its engine has fractured. Just a temporary stop, though it may take some hours to repair. But there's no cause for worry, and half-hourly reports on the state of repairs should be forthcoming."

Another disturbing point had arisen: Lord Worth disclosed that no major marine-insurance companies or Lloyd's of London had ever heard of the existence of the *Tiburon*. The fact was less than surprising if one knew of Mulhooney's re-naming exploits—*Hammond* to *Tiburon* to

Georgia. The vessel had virtually ceased to exist. Even more disturbing, however, was the fact that the Marine Gulf Corporation had reported the disappearance of its seismological survey vessel from Freeport. It was called the *Hammond.*

The U. S. Navy had two points of cold comfort to offer. What the United States did with its obsolete submarines was to scrap them or sell them to foreign governments: none had ever fallen into the hands of commercial companies or private individuals. Nor were there any Cousteau-type submersibles along the Gulf Coast.

The telephone bell jangled. Lord Worth switched on the wall receivers. The radio officer was succinct.

"Helicopter, flying low, due northwest, five miles out."

"Well, now," Larsen said, "this should provide a diversion. Coming, Mitchell?"

"In a minute. I have a little note to write. Remember?"

"The note, of course." Larsen left. Mitchell penned a brief note in neat printed script that left no room for misinterpretation, folded it in his pocket and went to the door. Lord Worth said: "Mind if I come along?"

"Well, there won't be any danger, but I think you'd do better to listen for messages from radar, radio, sonar and so forth."

"Agreed. And I'll call up the Secretary to see

what luck he's had in hauling those damned warships off my back."

Marina said sweetly: "If there's no danger I'm coming with you."

"No."

"You have a very limited vocabulary, Mr. Mitchell."

"Instead of trying to be a heroine you might try the Florence Nightingale bit—there are two very sick people through there who need their hands held."

"You're much too bossy, Michael."

"As they say, a male chauvinist pig."

"Could you imagine me marrying a person like you?"

"Your imagination is your own business. Besides, I've never asked you to." He left.

"Well!" She looked suspiciously at her father, but Lord Worth had his risibility under complete control. He picked up a phone and asked that the Christmas tree be opened and the exploratory drilling restarted.

The helicopter was making its landing approach as Mitchell joined Larsen and Palermo and his men in the deep shadows of the accommodation area. The platform light had been dimmed but the helipad was brightly illuminated. Palermo had six portable searchlights in position. He nodded to Mitchell, then made his unhurried way to the pad. He was carrying an envelope in his hand.

The helicopter touched down, the door opened and men with a discouraging assortment of automatic weapons started to disembark. Palermo said: "I'm Marino. Who's in charge here?"

"Me. Mortensen." He was a bulky young man in battle fatigues, looking more like a bright young lieutenant than the thug he undoubtedly was. "I thought Durand was in charge here."

"He is. Right now he's having a talk with Lord Worth. He's waiting for you in Worth's quarters."

"Why are the deck lights so dim?"

"Voltage drop. Being fixed. The landing pads have their own generators." He pointed. "Over there."

Mortensen nodded and led his eight men away. Palermo said: "Be with you in a minute. I've got a private message for the pilot from Cronkite."

Palermo climbed up into the helicopter. He greeted the pilot and said: "I got a message here for you from Cronkite."

The pilot registered a degree of surprise. "I was told to fly straight back."

"Won't be long. Seems Cronkite is anxious to see Worth and his daughters."

The pilot grinned and took the envelope from Palermo. He opened it, examined both sides of a blank sheet of paper and said: "What gives?"

"This." Palermo showed him a gun about the size of a small cannon. "Don't be a dead hero."

The platform lights went out and six searchlights came on. Larsen's stentorian voice carried clearly. "Throw down your guns. You haven't got a chance."

One of Mortensen's men suicidally thought different. He flung himself to the platform deck, loosed off a burst of submachine fire and successfully killed one of the searchlights. If he felt any sense of gratification it must have been the shortest on record, for he was dead before the shattered glass stopped tinkling down on the platform. The other eight men threw down their guns.

Palermo sighed. He said to the pilot: "See? Dead heroes are no good to anyone. Come on."

Eight of the nine men, including the pilot, were shepherded into a windowless storeroom and locked inside. The ninth, Mortensen, was taken to the radio room where he was shortly joined by Mitchell. For the occasion, Mitchell had changed into a boiler suit and makeshift hood, which not only effectively masked his face but also muffled his voice. He had no wish to be identified.

He produced the paper on which he had made notes, screwed the muzzle of his .38 into the base of Mortensen's neck, told him to contact Cronkite and read out the message and that the slightest deviation from the script would mean a shattered brain. Mortensen was no fool and in his peculiar line of trade he had looked into the face of death more than once. He made the contact, said all was well, that he and Durand were in complete control of the *Seawitch,* but that it might be several hours before the helicopter could return, as last-minute engine failure had damaged the undercarriage. Cronkite seemed reasonably satisfied and hung up.

When Larsen and Mitchell returned to Lord Worth's cabin the latter seemed in a more cheerful frame of mind. The Pentagon had reported that the two naval vessels from Cuba and the one from Venezuela were stopped in the water and appeared to be waiting instructions. The *Torbello* was on its way again and was expected to arrive in Galveston in ninety minutes. Lord Worth might have felt less satisfied if he'd known that the *Torbello,* shaking in every rivet, seam and plate, was several hundred miles from Galveston, traveling southwest in calm seas. Mulhooney was in no mood to hang around.

Marina said accusingly: "I heard shots being fired out there."

"Just warning shots in the air," Mitchell said. "Scares the hell out of people."

"You made them all prisoner."

Lord Worth said irritably: "Don't talk nonsense. Now do be quiet. The commander and I have important matters to discuss."

"We'll leave," Mitchell said. He looked at Marina. "Come on—let's see the patients off."

They followed the two stretchers out to the helicopter. They were accompanied by Durand and Aaron—both with their hands tied behind their backs and on a nine-inch hobble—Dr. Greenshaw and one of Palermo's men, a menacing individual with a sawed-off shotgun who was to ride guard on the captives until they reached the mainland.

Mitchell said to Marina: "Last chance."

"No."

"We're going to make a great couple," Mitchell said gloomily. "Monosyllabic, yet."

They said their goodbyes, watched the helicopter lift off and made their way back to Lord Worth's quarters. Both Worth and Larsen were on separate lines, and from the expressions on their faces it was clear that they were less happy with life than they might have been. Both men were trying, with zero effect, to obtain some additional tankerage. There were, in fact, some half-dozen idle tankers on the south and east coasts in the 50,000-ton range, but all belonged to the major oil companies, who would have gone to the stake before chartering any of their vessels to the North Hudson Oil Company. The nearest tankers of the required tonnage were either in Britain, Norway or the Mediterranean, and to have brought them across would have involved an intolerable loss of time, not to say money—this last matter lying very close to Lord Worth's heart. He and Larsen had even considered bringing one of their supertankers into service, but had decided against it. Because of the tankers' huge carrying capacity, the loss in revenue would have been unbearably high—and what had happened to the *Crusader* might happen to a supertanker. True, they were insured at Lloyd's, but that august firm's marine-accident investigators were notoriously, if justifiably, cagey, prudent and cautious men; and although they invariably settled any genuine claim, they tended to deliberate at length before making any final decision.

Another call came through from the *Torbello*. On course, its estimated time of arrival in Galveston was one hour. Lord Worth said gloomily that they had at least two tankers in operation: they would just have to step up their already crowded schedules.

One half hour later another message came through from the tanker. One half hour to Galveston. Lord Worth might have felt less assured had he known that now that dark had fallen, the *Starlight*, leaving the *Georgia* where it was, had already moved away in the direction of the *Seawitch*, its engines running on its electrical batteries. Its chances of sonar detection by the *Seawitch* were regarded as extremely small. It carried with it highly skilled divers and an unpleasant assortment of mines, limpet mines and amatol beehives, all of which could be activated by remote radioactive control.

Yet another half hour passed before the welcome news came through that the tanker *Torbello* was safely berthed in Galveston. Lord Worth informed Larsen he intended to make an immediate voice-link call to the port authorities in Galveston to ensure the fastest turnaround ever, money no object.

He got his voice link in just one minute—the Lord Worths of this world are never kept waiting. When he made his customary peremptory demands the harbormaster expressed a considerable degree of surprise.

"I really don't know what you're talking about, sir."

"Goddam it, I always know what I'm talking about."

"Not in this case, Lord Worth. I'm afraid you've been misinformed or hoaxed. The *Torbello* has not arrived."

"But dammit, I've just heard—"

"One moment, please."

The moment passed into about thirty during which Mitchell thoughtfully brought Lord Worth a glass of scotch, which he half-consumed at one gulp. Then the voice came through again.

"Bad news. There's not only no sign of your

tanker, but our radar scanners show no signs of any vessel of that size within a radius of forty miles."

"Then, what the devil can have happened to her? I was speaking to her only two or three minutes ago."

"On her own call sign?"

"Yes, dammit."

"Then obviously she's in no trouble."

Lord Worth hung up without as much as a courtesy thank you. He glowered at Larsen and Mitchell as if what had happened had been their fault. He said at length: "I can only conclude that the captain of the *Torbello* has gone off his rocker."

Mitchell said: "And I conclude that he's under lock and key aboard his own ship."

Lord Worth was heavily ironic. "In addition to your many other accomplishments you've now become psychic."

"Your *Torbello* has been hijacked."

"Hijacked! Hijacked? Now *you've* gone off your rocker. Who ever heard of a tanker being hijacked?"

"Who ever heard of a jumbo jet being hijacked until the first one was? After what happened to the *Crusader* in Galveston, the captain of the *Torbello* would have been extremely leery of being approached, much less boarded, by any other vessel unless it were a craft with respectability beyond question. The only two such types of craft are naval or coast guard. We've heard that the Marine Gulf Corporation's survey vessel has been stolen. A lot of those survey vessels are ex-coast guard with landing space for a helicopter to carry out seismological pattern bombing. That ship was called the *Hammond*. With your connections you could find out about it in minutes."

Lord Worth did find out in minutes. He said: "So you're right." He was too dumbfounded even to apologize. "And this of course was the *Tiburon* that Cronkite sailed from Galveston. God only knows what name it goes under now. What next, I wonder?"

Mitchell said: "A call from Cronkite, I'd guess."

"What would he call me for?"

"Some tough demands, I'd say. I don't know."

Lord Worth was nothing if not resilient. He had powerful and influential friends. He called an admiral in naval headquarters in Washington and demanded that an air-sea search unit be dispatched immediately to the scene. The Navy apologetically said that they would have to obtain the permission of the Commander-in-Chief —that is, the President. The President, he knew, would profess a profound if polite degree of disinterest. Neither he nor Congress had any reason to love the oil companies who had so frequently flouted them—which was less than fair to Lord Worth, who had never flouted anyone in Washington in his life. More, the search almost certainly lay outside their jurisdictional waters. Besides, it was raining in the Gulf and black as the pit, and though their radar might well pick up a hundred ships in the area, visual identification would be impossible.

He tried the CIA. Their disinterest was even more profound. In the several years past they had had their fingers badly burned in public and all their spare time was devoted to licking their wounds.

The FBI curtly reminded him that their activities were purely internal and that anyway they got seasick whenever they ventured on water.

Lord Worth considered making an appeal to the UN, but was dissuaded by Larsen and Mitchell. Not only would the Arab states, Venezuela, Nigeria, every Communist country, and what now went by the name of the Third World—and they held the vast majority of votes in the UN— veto any such suggestion: the UN had no legal power to initiate any such action. Apart from that, by that time the entire UN complex were probably in bed anyway.

For once in his life, Lord Worth appeared to be at a loss. Life, it appeared, could hold no more for him. Lord Worth was discovering that, upon occasion, he could be as fallible as the next man.

A voice-over call came through. It was, as Mitchell had predicted it would be, Cronkite. He was glad to inform Lord Worth that there was no cause for concern over the *Torbello,* as she was in safe and sound hands.

"Where?" Had his daughter not been present, Lord Worth would undoubtedly have qualified his question with a few choice adjectives.

"I prefer not to specify exactly. Enough to say that she is securely anchored in the territorial waters of a Central American country. It is my intention to dispose of this oil to this very poor and oil-deficient country"—he did not mention that it was his intention to sell it at half price, which would bring in a few acceptable hundred thousands of dollars—"then take the tanker out to sea and sink it. Unless, of course—"

"Unless what?" Lord Worth asked. His voice had assumed a peculiar hoarseness.

"Unless you close down the Christmas tree on the *Seawitch* and immediately stop all pumping and drilling."

"Fool."

"How's that?"

"Your thugs have already attended to that. Haven't they told you?"

"I want proof. I want Mortensen."

Lord Worth said wearily: "Hold on. We'll get him."

Mitchell went to fetch him. By the time he returned, overalled and masked, Mortensen had been thoroughly briefed. He confirmed to Cronkite that all pumping and drilling had stopped. Cronkite expressed his satisfaction and the radio link went dead. Mitchell removed the .38 from below Mortensen's ear and two of Palermo's men took him from the room. Mitchell took off his hood and Marina looked at him with a mixture of horror and incredulity.

She whispered: "You were ready to kill him."

"Not at all. I was going to pat him on the head and tell him what a good boy he was. I asked you to get off this rig."

Chapter 9

LORD Worth had barely begun to wipe his brow when two men hurried into the room. One was Palermo and the other was one of the rig crew, Simpson, whose duty it was to monitor the sensory instruments attached to the platform's legs and the tensioning anchor cables. He was obviously in a state of considerable agitation.

Lord Worth said: "What fresh horror does fate hold in store for us now?"

"Somebody below the rig, sir. My instruments have gone a bit haywire. Some object, almost certainly metallic, is in intermittent contact with the western leg."

"There can be no doubt about this?" Simpson shook his head. "Seems damnably odd that Cronkite would try to bring down the *Seawitch* with his own men on board."

Mitchell said: "Maybe he doesn't want to bring it down, just damage the leg enough to destroy the buoyancy in the leg and the adjacent members and tilt the *Seawitch* so the drill and pumping mechanisms don't work. Maybe anything. Or maybe he would be prepared to sacrifice his own men to get you." He turned to Palermo. "I know you've got scuba equipment aboard. Show me." They left.

Marina said: "I suppose he's off to murder someone else. He's not really human, is he?"

Lord Worth looked at her without enthusiasm. "If you call being inhuman wanting to see that you don't die, then he's inhuman. There's only one person aboard this rig he really cares for, and you damned well know it. I never thought I'd be ashamed of a daughter of mine."

Palermo had, in fact, two trained scuba divers with him, but Mitchell chose only one to accompany him. Palermo was not a man to be easily impressed, but he had seen enough of Mitchell not to question his judgment. In remarkably quick time Mitchell and the other man, who went by the name of Sawyers, were dressed in scuba outfits and were equipped with reloadable compressed-air harpoon guns and sheath knives.

They were lowered to the water by the only available means on such a giant TLP—a wire-mesh cage attached to the boom of the derrick crane. At water level they opened the hinged door, dived and swam to the giant western leg.

Simpson had made no mistake. They were indeed at work down there, two of them, attached by airlines and cables to the shadowy outline of a vessel some twenty feet above them. Both wore powerful headlamps. They were energetically engaged in attaching limpet mines, conventional magnetic mines and wraparound rolls of beehive amatol to the enormous leg. They had enough explosives there, Mitchell figured, to bring down the Eiffel Tower. Maybe Cronkite did intend to destroy the leg. That Cronkite was unhinged seemed more probable than not.

The two saboteurs were not only energetically engaged in their task, they were so exclusively preoccupied with it that they failed to notice the stealthy approach of Mitchell and Sawyers. The two scuba divers pressed their masks together, looked into each other's eyes—there was sufficient reflected light from the other divers to allow them to do this—and nodded simultaneously. Not much given to squeamishness where potential killers were concerned, they harpooned the two saboteurs through their backs. In both cases, death was instantaneous. Mitchell and Sawyers reloaded their compressed-air harpoons then, for good measure, sliced their two victims' breathing tubes, which also contained the communication wires.

On the *Starlight*, Easton and his crew were instantly aware that something had gone drastically wrong. The dead men were pulled up, the harpoons still imbedded in their backs, and as the corpses were being hauled over the gunwales two of the crew cried out in agony: Mitchell and Sawyers had surfaced and picked off two more targets. Whether either had been mortally or grievously injured was impossible to say, but far more than enough had happened for Easton to take off at speed, this time on his much faster diesels: the engines were admittedly noisy, but the darkness was so intense that it was impossible for the alerted gunners on the platform to obtain an accurate fix on them.

The two scuba divers, their own headlights now switched on, swam down to the spot where the mines and explosives had been attached to the legs. There were time fuses attached to both mines and explosives. Those they detached and let fall to the bottom of the ocean. For good measure they also removed the detonators. The explosives, now harmless, they unwound and let them follow the time fuses. The mines they prudently left where they were. Both men were explosives experts but not deep-water explosives experts. Mines, as many ghosts can attest, can be very tricky and unpredictable. They consist of TNT, amatol, or some such conventional explosive as the main charge. In their central tube they have a primer, which may consist of one of a variety of slow-burning explosives, and fitted to the top of the primer is a traveling detonator, activated by sea pressure, which usually consists of seventy-seven grains of fulminate of mercury. Even with this detonator removed, the primer can still detonate under immense pressure. Neither diver had any wish to blow up the pile-driven anchors or the tensioning cables attached to the anchors. Via the derrick crane they made their way back to the platform and reported to the radio room. They had to wait for some time before making their report, for Lord Worth was in a far from amicable telephone conversation with Cronkite. Marina sat apart, her hands clenched and her normally tanned face a grayish color. She looked at Mitchell, then averted her eyes as if she never wished to set eyes on him again, which, at the moment, she probably didn't.

Cronkite was furious. "You murderous bastard, Worth." He was clearly unaware that he was talking in the presence of ladies. "Three of my men dead, harpooned through the back." Involuntarily, Marina looked at Mitchell again. Mitchell had the impression that he was either a monster from outer space or from the nethermost depths: at any rate, a monster.

Lord Worth was no less furious. "It would be a pleasure to repeat the process—with you as the central figure this time."

Cronkite choked, then said with what might have been truth: "My intention was just temporarily to incapacitate the *Seawitch* without harming anyone aboard. But if you want to play it rough you'll have to find a new *Seawitch* in twenty-four hours. That's if you're fortunate enough to survive: I'm going to blast you out of the water."

Lord Worth was calmer now. "It would be interesting to know how you're going to achieve that. My information is that your warships have been ordered back to base."

"There's more than one way of blasting you out of the water." Cronkite sounded very sure of himself. "In the meantime I'm going to offload the *Torbello*'s oil, then sink it." In point of fact, Cronkite had no intention of sinking the tanker: the *Torbello* was a Panamanian registered tanker, and Cronkite was not lacking in Panamanian friends. A tanker could be easily disposed of for a very considerable sum. The conversation, if such an acrimonious exchange could be so called, ended abruptly.

Mitchell said: "One thing's for sure. Cronkite is a fluent liar. He's nowhere near Central America. Not with that kind of reception. And we heard him talking to his friend Durand. He elected not to come on that helicopter flight—

which lasted only fifteen minutes. He's lying out there somewhere just over the horizon."

Lord Worth said: "How did things go down there?"

"You heard what Cronkite said. There was no trouble on our part."

"Do you expect more?"

"Yeah. Cronkite sounds too damn confident for me."

"How do you think it'll come?"

"Your guess is as good as mine. He might even try the same thing again."

Lord Worth was incredulous. "After what happened to him?"

"He may be counting on the unexpected. One thing I'm sure of. If he does try the same again he'll use different tactics. I'm sure he won't try an air or submarine approach, if for no other reason than that he doesn't—he can't—have skilled men. So I don't think you'll need your radar or sonar watchers tonight. In any case, your radio operator may need a rest—after all, he's got an alarm call-up in his cabin. I'd keep Simpson on duty, though. Just in case our friends try for one of the legs again."

Palermo said: "But they'd be waiting this time. They'd be operating close to the surface. They'd have armed guards waiting to protect the divers, maybe even infrared searchlights that we couldn't see from the platform. You and Sawyers were lucky the first time, and luck depends on surprise: but there wouldn't be any surprise this time."

"We don't need luck. Lord Worth wouldn't have had all those depth charges stolen and brought aboard unless one of your men is an expert in depth charges. You've got such a man?"

"Yeah." Palermo eyed him speculatively. "Cronin. Ex-petty officer. Why?"

"He could arrange the detonator setting so that the depth charge would explode immediately or soon after hitting the water?"

"I guess so. Again, why?"

"We roll three depth charges along the platform to within, say, twenty-five yards of each of the legs. Your friend Cronin could advise us on this. My distance could be wrong. If Simpson detects anything on his sensors we just push one of the depth charges over the side. The blast effect should have no effect on the leg. I doubt if the boat with the divers would get anything more than a hard shaking. But for divers in the water the concussive shock effects could hardly miss being fatal."

Palermo looked at him with cold appraising eyes. "For a man supposed to be on the side of the law, Mitchell, you're the most cold-blooded bastard I've ever met."

"If you want to die just say so. You'd find it a bit uncomfortable nine hundred feet down in the Gulf. I suggest you get Cronin and a couple of your men and get going on the depth charges."

Mitchell followed to watch Palermo, Cronin and two of their men at work. Cronin agreed with Mitchell's estimate of placing the depth charges twenty-five yards from the legs. As he stood there Marina came up to him.

She said: "More men are going to die, aren't they, Michael?"

"I hope not."

"But you are getting ready to kill, aren't you?"

"I'm getting ready to survive. I'm getting ready for all of us to survive."

She took his arm. "Do you like killing?"

"No."

"Then how come you're so good at it?"

"Somebody has to be."

"For the good of mankind, I suppose?"

"Look, you don't have to talk to me." He paused and went on slowly. "Cops kill. Soldiers kill. Airmen kill. They don't have to like it. In the First World War a guy named Marshal Foch got to be the most decorated soldier of the war for being responsible for the deaths of a million men. The fact that most of them were his own men would seem to be beside the point. I don't hunt, I don't shoot game, I don't even fish. I mean, I like lamb as much as the next man, but I wouldn't put a hook in one's throat and drag it around a field for half an hour before it dies from agony and exhaustion. All I do is exterminate vermin. To me, all crooks, armed or not, are vermin."

"Is that why you and John got fired from the police?"

"Do I have to tell you that?"

"Have you ever killed what you, what I, would call a good person?"

"No. But unless you shut up——"

"In spite of everything, I think I might still marry you."

"I've never asked you."

"Well, what are you waiting for?"

Mitchell sighed, then smiled. "Marina Worth, would you do me the honor——"

Behind them, Lord Worth coughed. Marina swung round. "Daddy," she said, "you have a genius for turning up at the wrong moment."

Lord Worth was mild. "The right moment I would have said. My unreserved congratulations." He looked at Mitchell. "Well, you certainly took your time about it. Everything shipshape and secured for the night?"

"As far as I can guess at what goes on in Cronkite's mind."

"My confidence in you, my boy, is total. Well, it's bed for me—I feel, perhaps not unaccountably, extremely tired."

Marina said: "Me, too. Well, goodnight, fiancé." She kissed him lightly and left with her father.

For once, Lord Worth's confidence in Mitchell was slightly misplaced. The latter had made a mistake, though a completely unwitting one, in sending the radio officer off duty. For had that officer remained on duty he would undoubtedly have picked up the news flash about the theft of the nuclear weapons from the Netley Rowan Arsenal: Mitchell could not have failed to put two and two together.

During the third hour of Lord Worth's conscience-untroubled sleep Mulhooney had been extremely active. He had discharged his fifty thousand tons of oil and taken the *Torbello* well out to sea, far over the horizon. He returned later with two companions in the ship's only motorized lifeboat with the sad news that, in the sinking of the tanker, a shattering explosion had occurred which had decimated his crew. They three were the only survivors. The decimated crew were, at that moment, taking the *Torbello* south to Panama. The official condolences were widespread, apparently sincere and wholly hypocritical: when a tanker blows up its motorized lifeboat does not survive intact. The republic had no diplomatic relations with the United States, and the only things they would cheerfully have extradited to that country were cholera and the bubonic plague. A private jet awaited the three at the tiny airport. Passports duly stamped, Mulhooney and his friends filed a flight plan for Guatemala.

Some hours later they arrived at the Houston International Airport. With much of the ten million dollars still remaining at his disposal, Cronkite was not the man to worry about incidental expenses. Mulhooney and his friends immediately hired a long-range helicopter and set out for the Gulf.

In the fourth hour of his sleep, which had remained undisturbed by the sound of a considerable underwater explosion, Lord Worth was unpleasantly awakened by a call from a seethingly mad Cronkite, who accused him of killing two more of his men and warned that he was going to extract a fearful vengeance. Lord Worth hung up without bothering to reply, sent for Mitchell and learned that Cronkite had indeed made another attempt to sabotage the western leg. The depth charge had apparently done everything expected of it, for their searchlights had picked up the bodies of two divers floating on the surface. The craft that had been carrying them could not have been seriously damaged for they had heard the sound of its diesels starting up. Instead of making a straight escape, it had disappeared under the rig, and by the time they had crossed to the other side of the *Seawitch* it was long gone into the darkness and rain. Lord Worth smiled happily and went back to sleep.

In the fifth hour of his sleep he would not have been smiling quite so happily if he had been aware of certain strange activities that were taking place in a remote Louisiana motel, one exclusively owned by Lord Worth himself. Here it was that the *Seawitch*'s relief crews spent their time off in the strictest seclusion. In addition to abundant food, drink, films, TV and a high-class bordello, it offered every amenity off-duty oil-rig men could ever have wished for. Not that any of them would have wanted to leave the compound gates anyway: nine out of ten of them were wanted by the law, and total privacy was a paramount requirement.

The intruders, some twenty in all, arrived in the middle of the night. They were led by a man named Gregson: of all Cronkite's associates, he was by far the most dangerous and lethal and was possessed of the morality and instincts of a fer-de-lance with a toothache. The motel staff were all asleep and were chloroformed before they had any opportunity of regaining consciousness.

The rig relief crew, also, were all asleep but in a somewhat different fashion and for different reasons. Liquor is forbidden on oil rigs, and the relief crews on the night before returning to duty generally made the best of their last chance. Their dormant states ranged from the merely befuddled to the paralytic. The rounding up of them, most of whom remained still asleep on their feet, took no more than five minutes. The only two relatively sober members of the relief crew tried to offer resistance. Gregson, with a silenced Beretta, gunned them down as if they had been wild dogs.

The captives were transported in a completely standard, albeit temporarily purloined, moving van to an abandoned and very isolated warehouse on the outskirts of town. Somewhat less than salubrious, it was perfectly fitted for Gregson's purpose. The prisoners were neither bound nor gagged, which would have been pointless in the presence of two armed guards who carried the customary intimidating machine carbines. In point of fact, the carbines too were superfluous: the besotted captives had already drifted off into a dreamless slumber.

It was in the sixth hour of Lord Worth's equally dreamless slumber that Gregson and his men lifted off in one of Lord Worth's helicopters. The two pilots had been reluctant to accept them as passengers, but Schmeissers are powerfully persuasive agents.

It was in the seventh hour of Lord Worth's slumber that Mulhooney and his two colleagues touched down on the empty helipad of the *Georgia*. As Cronkite's own helicopter was temporarily marooned on the *Seawitch,* he had no compunction in impounding both the helicopter and its hapless pilot.

At almost exactly the same moment another

helicopter touched down on the *Seawitch* and a solitary passenger and pilot emerged. The passenger was Dr. Greenshaw, and he looked, and was, a very tired elderly man. He went straight to the sick bay and, without even trying to remove his clothes, lay down on one of the cots and composed himself for sleep. He should, he supposed, have reported to Lord Worth that his daughter Melinda and John Roomer were in good hands and good shape, but good news could wait.

On the eighth hour, with the dawn in the sky, Lord Worth, a man who enjoyed his sleep, awoke, stretched himself luxuriously, pulled on his splendidly embroidered dressing gown and strolled out onto the platform. The rain had stopped, the sun was tipping the horizon and there was every promise of a beautiful day to come. Privately congratulating himself on his prescience that no trouble would occur during the night, he retired to his quarters to perform his customary and leisurely morning ablutions.

Lord Worth's self-congratulations on his prescience were entirely premature. Fifteen minutes earlier the radio operator, newly returned to duty, had picked up a news broadcast that he didn't like at all and gone straight to Mitchell's room. Like every man on board, even including Larsen and Palermo, he knew that the man to contact in an emergency was Mitchell: the thought of alerting Lord Worth never entered his head.

He found Mitchell shaving. Mitchell looked tired—less than surprising, as he had spent most of the night awake. Mitchell said: "No more trouble, I hope?"

"I don't know." He handed Mitchell a strip of teletype. It read: "Two tactical nuclear weapons stolen from the Netley Rowan Arsenal yesterday afternoon. Intelligence suspects they are being flown or helicoptered south over Gulf of Mexico to an unknown destination. A worldwide alert has been issued. Anyone able to provide information should—"

"Jesus! Get hold of this arsenal any way you can. Use Lord Worth's name. Be with you in a minute."

Mitchell was with him in half a minute. The operator said: "I'm through already. Not much co-operation, though."

"Give me that phone. My name's Mitchell. Who's speaking, please?"

"Colonel Pryce." The tone wasn't exactly distant, just a senior officer talking to a civilian.

"I work for Lord Worth. You can check that with the Fort Lauderdale Police, the Pentagon or the Secretary of State." He said to the operator but loudly enough that Pryce could hear: "Get Lord Worth here. I don't care if he's in his damned bath, just get him here now." Back on the phone, he said: "Colonel Pryce, an officer of your grade should know that Lord Worth's daughters have been kidnaped. I was hired to recover them and I did so. More important, this oil rig, the *Seawitch,* is now under threat of destruction. Two attempts have already been made. They were unsuccessful. The Pentagon will confirm that they've stopped three foreign warships headed here for the purpose of destroying the *Seawitch.* I believe those nukes weapons are heading this way. I want full information about them and I'll warn you that Worth will interpret any failure to provide this information as a gross dereliction of duty. And you know the clout that Lord Worth has."

There was a far from subtle change in Colonel Pryce's tone. "It's quite unnecessary to threaten me."

"Just a minute. Lord Worth's just arrived." Mitchell gave a brief resume of his phone conversation, making sure that Pryce could hear every word.

"Nuclear bloody bombs! That's why Cronkite said he could blast us out of the water!" Lord Worth snatched the phone from Mitchell. "Worth here. I have a hotline to the Secretary of State, Dr. Benton. I could patch him in in fifteen seconds. Do you want me to do that?"

"That will not be necessary, Lord Worth."

Alistair MacLean

"Then give us a detailed description of those damned things and tell us how they work."

Pryce, almost eagerly, gave the description. It was almost precisely similar to the one that Captain Martin had given to the bogus Colonel Farquharson. "But Martin was a new officer and shaky on his details. The nuclear devices—you can hardly call them bombs—are probably twice as effective as he said. They took the wrong type —those devices have no black button to shut off in emergency. And they have a ninety-minute setting, not sixty. *And* they can be radio-activated."

"Something complicated? I mean, a VHF number or something of the kind?"

"Something very uncomplicated. You can't expect a soldier in the heat of battle to remember abstruse numbers. It's simply a pear-shaped device with a plastic seal. Strip that off and turn a black switch through three hundred and sixty degrees. It's important to remember that turning this switch off will deactivate the detonating mechanism in the device. It can be turned on again at any time."

"If it should be used against us . . . we have a huge oil-storage tank nearby. Wouldn't this cause a massive oil slick?"

"Sir—oil is by nature combustible and much more easily vaporized than steel."

"Thank you."

"Seems to me you need a squadron of supersonic fighter-bombers out there. I'll relay the request, but they'll have to get Pentagon permission first."

"Thank you again."

Lord Worth and Mitchell left for the former's quarters. Lord Worth said: "Two things. We're only assuming, although it would be dangerous not to assume, that those damned things are meant for us. Besides, if we keep our radar, sonar and sensory posts manned I don't see how Cronkite could approach and deliver them."

"It's hard to see how. But then, it's harder to figure out that bastard's turn of mind."

From Lord Worth's helicopter Gregson made contact with the *Georgia*. "We're fifteen miles out."

Cronkite himself replied, "We'll be airborne in ten."

A wall radio crackled in Lord Worth's room. "Helicopter approaching from the northeast."

"No sweat. Relief crew."

Lord Worth had gone back to his shower when the relief helicopter touched down. Mitchell was in his laboratory, looking very professional in his white coat and glasses. Dr. Greenshaw was still asleep.

Apart from gagging and manacling the pilots, the helicopter passengers had offered them no violence. They disembarked in quiet and orderly fashion. The drill duty crew observed their arrival without any particular interest. They had been well-trained to mind their own business and had highly personal reasons for not fraternizing with unknowns. And the new arrivals were unknowns. Off the coast Lord Worth owned no fewer than nine oil rigs—all legally leased and paid for—and for reasons best known to his devious self he was in the habit of regularly rotating his drill crews. The new arrivals carried the standard shoulder-slung clothesbags. Those bags did indeed contain a minimal amount of clothes, but not clothing designed to be worn: the clothes were there merely to conceal and muffle the shape of the machine pistols and other more deadly weapons in the bags.

Thanks to the instructions he had received from Cronkite via Durand, Gregson knew exactly where to go. He noted the presence of two idly patrolling guards and marked them down for death.

He led his men to the oriental quarters, where they laid their bags on the platform and unzipped them. Windows were smashed and what followed was sheer savage massacre. Within half a dozen seconds of machine-gun fire, bazooka fire and incinerating flamethrowers, all of which had been preceded by a flurry of tear-gas bombs, all screaming inside had ceased. The two advancing guards were mown down even as they drew their guns. The only survivor was Larsen, who had been in his own private room in the back: Palermo and all his men were dead.

Figures appeared almost at the same instant from the quarters at the end of the block. Sound-proofed though those quarters were, the noise outside had been too penetrating not to be heard. There were four of them—two men in white coats, a man in a Japanese kimono and a black-haired guard in a wrap. One of Gregson's men fired twice at the nearest white-coated figure, and Mitchell staggered and fell backward to the deck. Gregson brutally smashed the wrist of the man who had fired, who screamed in agony as the gun fell from his shattered hand.

"You bastard idiot!" Gregson's voice was as vicious as his appearance. "The hard men only, Mr. Cronkite said."

Gregson was nothing if not organized. He de-tailed five groups of two men. One group herded the drilling-rig crew into the occidental quarters. The second, third and fourth went respectively to the sensory room, the sonar room and the radar room. There they tied up but did not otherwise harm the operators, before they rid-dled all the equipment with a burst of machine-gun bullets. For all practical purposes, the *Seawitch* was now blind, deaf and benumbed. The fifth group went to the radio room, where the operator was tied up but his equipment left intact.

Dr. Greenshaw approached Gregson. "You are the leader?"

"Yes."

"I'm a doctor." He nodded to Mitchell, whose white coat accentuated the stains of his blood and was rolling about in a convincing manner, Marina bending over him with bitter tears rolling down her cheeks. "He's hurt bad. I must take him into the sick bay and patch him up."

"We got no quarrel with you," Gregson said, which was, unwittingly, the most foolish remark he'd ever made.

Dr. Greenshaw helped the weak and staggering Mitchell into the sick bay, where, the door closed behind him, he made an immediate and remarkable recovery. Marina stared at him in astonishment, then in something approaching relieved ire.

"Why, you deceiving . . ."

"That's no way to talk to a wounded man." He was pulling off his white coat, coat and shirt. "I've never seen you cry before. Makes you look even more beautiful. And that's real blood." He turned to Dr. Greenshaw. "Superficial wound on the left shoulder, a scratch on the right forearm. Dead-eye Dick himself. Now do a real good job on me, Doc. Right arm bandaged from elbow to wrist. Left arm bandaged from shoulder to above the elbow with a great big sling. Marina, even ravishing beauties like you carry face powder. I hope you're no exception."

Not yet mollified, she said stiffly: "I have some. Baby powder," she added nastily.

"Get it, please."

Five minutes later, Mitchell had been rendered into the epitome of the walking wounded. His right arm was heavily bandaged and his left arm was swathed in white from shoulder to wrist. The sling was voluminous. His face was very pale. He left for his room and returned a few seconds later.

"Where have you been?" she asked suspiciously.

He reached inside the depths of the sling and pulled out his silenced .38. "Fully loaded." He returned it to its hiding place, where it was quite invisible.

"Never give up, do you?" Her voice held a curious mixture of awe and bitterness.

"Not when I'm about to be vaporized."

Dr. Greenshaw stared at him. "What do you mean?"

"Our friend Cronkite has heisted a couple of tactical nuclear weapons. He plans to finish off the *Seawitch* in Fourth of July style. He should be here about now. Now, Doc, I want you to do something for me. Take the biggest medical bag you have and tell Gregson that it is your humanitarian duty to go into the occidental quarters to help any of the dying, or, if necessary, put them out of their agony. I know they've got a fair supply of hand grenades in there. I want some."

"No sooner said than done. God, you look awful! Destroys my faith in myself as a doctor."

They went outside. Cronkite's helicopter was indeed just touching down. Cronkite himself was the first out, followed by Mulhooney, the three bogus officers who had stolen the nuclear weapons, the commandeered pilot and, lastly, Easton. Easton was the unknown quantity. Mitchell did not appreciate it at the time but Easton's *Starlight* had been so badly damaged by the depth charge that it was no longer serviceable. Less than four miles away what appeared to be a coast guard cutter was heading straight for the *Seawitch*. It required no guessing to realize that this was the missing *Hammond*, the infamous *Tiburon*, the present *Georgia*.

Dr. Greenshaw approached Gregson. "I'd like to have a look at what you've left of those quarters. Maybe there's someone still alive in there . . ."

Gregson pointed to an iron door. "I'm more interested in who's in there. Spicer"—this to one of his men—"a bazooka shot at that lock."

"That's hardly necessary," Greenshaw said mildly. "A knock from me is all that's needed. That's Commander Larsen, the boss of the oil rig. He's no enemy of yours. He just sleeps here because he likes his privacy." Dr. Greenshaw knocked. "Commander Larsen, it's okay. It's me, Greenshaw. Come on out. If you don't, there're some people who're going to blast your door down and you with it. Come on, man."

There was the turning of a heavy key and Larsen emerged. He looked dazed, almost shell-shocked, as well he might. He said: "What the hell goes on?"

"You've been taken over, friend," Gregson said. Larsen was dressed, Greenshaw was pleased to note, in a voluminous lumberjacket cinched at the waist. "Search him." They searched and found nothing.

"Where's Scoffield?" Larsen said.

Greenshaw said: "In the other quarters. He should be okay."

"Palermo?"

"Dead. And all his men. At least I think so. I'm just going to have a look." Stooping his shoulders to look more nearly eighty than seventy, Dr. Greenshaw shambled along the shattered corridor, but he could have saved himself the trouble of acting. Gregson had just met Cronkite outside the doorway and the two men were talking in animated and clearly self-congratulatory terms.

After the first few steps, Greenshaw realized that there could be nobody left alive in that charnel house. Those who were dead were very dead indeed, most of them destroyed beyond recognition, either cut up by machine-gun fire, shattered by bazookas or shriveled by the flamethrowers. But he did find the primary reason of his visit—a box of hand grenades in prime condition and a couple of Schmeisser subautomatics, fully loaded. A few of the grenades he stuffed into the bottom of his medical bag. He peered out one of the shattered windows at the back and found the area below in deep shadow. He carefully lowered some grenades to the platform and the two Schmeissers beside them. Then he made his way outside again.

It was apparent that Cronkite and Lord Worth had already met, although the meeting could not have been a normal one. Lord Worth was lying apparently senseless on his back, blood flowing from smashed lips and apparently broken nose, while both cheeks were badly bruised. Marina was bending over him, daubing at his wounds with a flimsy handkerchief. Cronkite, his face unmarked but his knuckles bleeding, had apparently, for the moment at least, lost interest in Lord Worth, no doubt waiting until Lord Worth had regained full consciousness before starting in on him again.

Lord Worth whispered between smashed lips: "Sorry, my darling; sorry, my beloved. My fault and all my fault. The end of the road."

"Yes." Her voice was as low as his own, but strangely there were no tears in her eyes. "But not for us. Not while Michael is alive."

Lord Worth looked at Michael through rapidly closing eyes. "What can a cripple like that do?"

She said quietly but with utter conviction: "He'll kill Cronkite and his whole mob."

He tried to smile through his smashed lips. "I thought you hated killing."

"Not vermin. Not people who do things like this to you."

Mitchell spoke quietly to Dr. Greenshaw, then both men approached Cronkite and Gregson, who broke off what appeared to be either a discussion or an argument. Dr. Greenshaw said: "You've done your damn murderous work all too well, Gregson. There's hardly a soul in there even recognizable as a human being."

Cronkite said: "Who's he?"

"A doctor."

Cronkite looked at Mitchell, who was looking worse by the minute. "And this?"

"A scientist. Shot by mistake."

"He's in great pain," Greenshaw said. "I've no X-ray equipment, but I suspect the arm's broken just below the shoulder."

Cronkite was almost jovial, the joviality of a man now almost detached from reality. "An hour from now he won't be feeling a thing."

Greenshaw said wearily: "I don't know what you mean. I want to take him back to the sick bay and give him a pain-killing injection."

"Why, sure: I want everyone to be fully prepared for what's about to happen."

"And what's that?"

"Later, later."

Greenshaw and the unsteady Mitchell moved off. They reached the sick bay, passed inside, went through the opposite side and made their unobserved way to the radio room. Greenshaw stood guard just inside the door while Mitchell, ignoring the bound operator, went straight to the transceiver. He raised the *Roamer* inside twenty seconds.

"Give me Captain Conde."

"Speaking."

"On your next circuit out to the oil tank get around behind it, then head south at full speed. The *Seawitch* has been taken over, but I'm sure there's nobody here who can operate the anti-aircraft guns. Stop at twenty miles and issue a general warning to all ships and aircraft not to approach within twenty miles of the *Seawitch*. You have its co-ordinates."

"Yes. But why——"

"Because there's going to be a mighty big bang. Christ's sake, don't argue."

"Don't argue about what?" a voice behind Mitchell said.

Mitchell turned round slowly. The man behind the pistol was smiling a smile that somehow lacked a genuine warmth. Greenshaw had been pushed to one side and the gun moved in a slow arc covering them both. "I got a hunch Gregson would like to see you both."

Mitchell rose, turned, half-staggered and clutched his right forearm inside the sling. Greenshaw said sharply: "God's sake, man, can't you see he's ill?"

The man glanced at Greenshaw for just a second, but a second was all that Mitchell required. The bullet from the silenced .38 took the gunman through the heart. Mitchell peered through the doorway. There was a fair degree of shadow there, no one in sight and the edge of the platform not more than twenty feet away. A few seconds later the dead man vanished over the edge. Mitchell and Greenshaw returned to the main body of the company via the sick bay. Cronkite and Gregson were still in deep discussion. Larsen stood some distance apart, apparently in a state of profound dejection. Greenshaw approached him and said quietly: "How do you feel?"

"How would you feel if you knew they intended to kill us all?"

"You'll feel better soon. Round the back of the building, when you get the chance, you'll find some hand grenades which should rest comfortably inside that lumberjacket of yours. You'll also find two loaded Schmeissers. I have a few grenades in my bag here. And Mitchell has his .38 inside his sling."

Larsen took care not to show his feelings. He looked as morose as ever. All he said was: "Boy, oh boy, oh boy."

Lord Worth was on his feet now, supported by his daughter. Mitchell joined them. "How do you feel?"

Lord Worth mouthed his words with understandable bitterness. "I'm in great shape."

"You'll feel better soon." He lowered his voice and spoke to Marina. "When I give the word, say you want to go to the ladies' room. But don't go there. Go to the generator room. You'll see a red lever there marked 'Deck Lights.' Pull it down. After you count twenty, throw it back on again."

Cronkite and Gregson appeared to have finished their discussion. From Cronkite's smile it appeared that his view had prevailed. Lord Worth, Marina, Larsen, Greenshaw and Mitchell stood together, a forlorn and huddled group. Facing them were the ranks of Cronkite, Mulhooney, Easton, and the bogus Colonel Farquharson, Lieutenant-Colonel Dewings, Major Breckley, Gregson and his killers, a formidable group and armed to the teeth.

Cronkite spoke to a man by his side. "Check."

The man lifted a walkie-talkie, spoke into it and nodded. He said to Cronkite: "Charges secured in position."

"Excellent. Tell them to go due north for twenty miles and stay there." This was done. Unfortunately for Cronkite, his view to the west was blocked by the shattered building behind him and he could not see that the *Roamer* was already proceeding steadily to the south.

Cronkite smiled. "Well, Worth, it's the end of the road for both you and the *Seawitch*." He dug into a pocket and produced a black pear-shaped metal container. "This is a radioactive detonating device. Note this small switch here. It's supposed to be good for sixty minutes, but I have already run off ten minutes of it. Fifty more minutes and poof: the *Seawitch*, you, Worth, and everyone aboard will be vaporized. Nobody's going to feel a thing, I assure you."

"You mean you intend to kill all my innocent employees aboard the rig? Cronkite, you are stark raving mad."

"Never saner. Can't have any witnesses left to identify us. Then we destroy two of the helicopters, cripple your derrick crane, smash your radio room and take off in the other two helicopters. You could, of course, figure on jumping into the Gulf, but your chances of survival would be about the same as a suicide jumping off the Golden Gate Bridge."

Mitchell nudged Marina. She said in a faint voice: "May I go to the ladies' room?"

Cronkite was joviality itself. " 'Course. But make it snappy."

Fifteen seconds later the deck lights went out.

In the end it was Mitchell, with his extraordinary capacity to see in the dark, who ran round the corner of the shattered building, retrieved the two Schmeissers—he didn't bother about the grenades—returned and thrust one into Larsen's hands. In eight seconds two men with submachine guns can achieve an extraordinary amount of carnage. Larsen was firing blind but Mitchell could see and pick out his targets. They were helped in a most haphazard fashion by Dr. Greenshaw, who flung grenades at random, inflicting even more damage on the already shattered building but not actually injuring anyone.

The lights came on again.

There were still seven people left alive—Cronkite, Mulhooney, Easton, Gregson and three of his men. To those seven Mitchell said: "All right, drop your guns." Shattered and stunned though the survivors were, they still had enough wits left to comply at once.

Marina arrived back and was promptly sick in a very unladylike fashion.

Mitchell put down his Schmeisser and advanced on Cronkite. "Give me that detonating device."

Cronkite removed it slowly from his pocket and lifted his arm preparatory to throwing it over the side. Whatever else, it would have meant the destruction of the *Seawitch*. Cronkite screamed in agony as the bullet from Mitchell's .38 shattered his right elbow. Mitchell caught the detonating device even before it could reach the deck.

He said to Larsen: "Are there two absolutely

secure places, with no windows and iron doors, which can be locked without any possibility of opening them from the inside?"

"Just two. Safe as Fort Knox vaults. Along here."

"Search these guys and search them thoroughly. Make sure they haven't even got a penknife."

Larsen searched. "Not even a penknife." He led them to a steel-reinforced cell-like structure and he and Mitchell ushered them inside.

In spite of his agony, Cronkite said: "You're not going to leave us in here, for God's sake!"

"Same as you were going to leave us." Mitchell paused, then added soothingly: "As you said, you won't feel a thing." He closed the door, double-locked it and put the key in his pocket. He said to Larsen: "The other cell?"

"Along here."

"This is madness!" Lord Worth's voice was almost a shout. "The *Seawitch* is safe now. Why in God's name destroy it?"

Mitchell ignored him. He glanced at the timing device on the detonator. "Twenty-nine minutes to go. We'd better move." He placed the device on the floor of the cell, locked the door and sent the key spinning far out over the Gulf. "Get the men out of the occidental buildings, and out of the sensory, radar, sonar and radio rooms and make sure that all the helicopter pilots are safe." He glanced at his watch. "Twenty-five minutes."

Everyone moved with alacrity except for Lord Worth, who merely stood with a stunned look on his face. Larsen said: "Do we need this mad rush?"

Mitchell said mildly: "How do we know that the settings on that detonator are accurate?"

The mad rush redoubled itself. Thirteen minutes before the deadline the last of the helicopters took off and headed south. The first to land on the *Roamer*'s helipad held Mitchell, Larsen, Lord Worth and his daughter, in addition to the doctor and several rig men, while the other helicopters still hovered overhead. They were still only about fourteen miles south of the *Seawitch*, which was as far as the *Roamer* had succeeded in getting. But Mitchell reckoned the margin of safety more than sufficient. He spoke to Conde, who assured him that every vessel and aircraft had been warned to keep as far away as possible from the danger area.

When the *Seawitch* blew up, dead on schedule, it did so with a spectacular effect that would have satisfied even the most ghoulish. There was even a miniature mushroom cloud such as the public had become accustomed to in the photographs of detonating atom bombs. Seventeen seconds later, those on the *Roamer* heard the thunderclap of sound, and shortly afterward a series of miniature but harmless tidal waves rocked but did not unduly disturb the *Roamer*.

After Mitchell had told Conde to broadcast the news to all aircraft and shipping, he turned to find a stony-faced Marina confronting him.

"Well, you've lost Daddy his *Seawitch*. I do hope you're satisfied with yourself."

"My, my, how bitter we are. Yes, it's a satisfactory job, even if I have to say it myself: obviously nobody else is going to."

"Why? Why? Why?"

"Every man who died there was a murderer, some of them mass murderers. They might have got away to countries with no extradition treaties with us. Even if they were caught, their cases might have dragged on for years. It would have been very difficult to get proof. And, of course, parole after a few years. This way, we know they'll never kill again."

"And it was worth it to destroy Daddy's pride and joy?"

"Listen, stupid. My father-in-law-to-be is—"

"That he'll never be." She was glaring at him.

"So okay. The old pirate is almost as big a crook as any of them. He associated with and hired for lethal purposes known criminals. He broke into two federal arsenals and mounted the equipment on the *Seawitch*. If the *Seawitch* had survived, federal investigators would have been aboard in an hour or so. He'd have got at least fifteen to twenty years in prison, and he'd probably have died in prison." Now her eyes were wide, with fear and understanding. "But now every last bit of evidence is at the bottom of the Gulf. Nothing can ever be traced against him."

"That's really why you vaporized the *Seawitch?*"

He eyed her affectionately. "Why should I admit anything to an ex-fiancée?"

"Mrs. Michael Mitchell." She mused. "I suppose I could go through life with a worse name."